A New Life For

Robert Johnson

by

Art Myers

2019

ISBN 978-1-7357208-2-1

Cover design by Janet L Blankenship

Contact Art Myers: artmyersbooks@gmail.com

For those that can do it and did.

Other Books* by Art Myers

MY STORY*
    How A Young Boy From California
        Ended Up An Old Man In Florida

ANDREW'S PIANO*

10,000 YEARS – Before Present*

ED ADAM CHASES A DREAM

*To my readers: The above books have been written, are in book format and planned to be published in 2021.

Chapter 1

Robert sat up, stretched, and tried to clear the sleep from his head. Looking around the now empty apartment he knew the nightmare was real. It was five-thirty in the morning Tuesday, March 31, 2015 and his world had just about come to an end. How so many things could have gone wrong in exactly one year didn't seem possible but today was to be his last day in San Francisco and he was not at all sure where he would be sleeping tonight. "Just one year. Jesus!" he thought.

He went into the bathroom, took a leak and avoided looking at himself in the mirror. The only good thing was that the apartment rent had included utilities and Wi-Fi so he was warm and could use his iPad, or he could once he set up his last eBay purchase which was thankfully delivered the day before. All the rented Rooms-to-Go furniture had been picked up yesterday and his small collection of dishes, silverware and cooking utensils were packed in one of four packing boxes sitting in the center of the empty living room. The other three contained the remainder of all his earthly possessions. Two suitcases and a hanger bag carried his clothes. It was a sad spectacle for a bachelor just one day short of his fortieth birthday.

"Jesus! How could all of this happened in just one

year?" he said out loud. No answer came so he walked over to the window that looked down on the entrance into the apartment's parking garage. His just purchased 2007 Honda Odyssey van was now in his parking space and was where the leased silver 2014 Porsche Carrera S use to reside. He took a hit on it's return, but at least he owned the Honda free and clear. There was room in the van for his boxes, suitcases, hangar bag, and the cheap air mattress he had slept on last night. There was always a Walmart parking lot to spend a night where ever he might be if that became necessary. What a depressing thought.

It all had started so good that Robert now thought that the gods had decided he should be punished. He had a degree in Computer Science from MIT and a Masters in Business from Stanford. He was not only smart but could reasonably think he was good looking. At least he had thought that a few months ago. Upon graduation at Stanford he had his choice of a number of positions and for some reason seemed to have chosen several bad ones early on. Silicon Valley was an easy place to do that, both in employment and in personal choices. He had entered the cycle of boom and bust with an emphasis on the bust leg. It was this last one that had really set him back. His first two jobs were just that, jobs. A good salary and benefits but lousy work which was most unsatisfactory for one of his talents. Then a small start up that didn't work out but which lead him into the arms of Engstrum Technologies. One year ago today, a Monday, March 31, 2014 was his first day as part of the team.

A substantial signing bonus, stock options and big salary. Plus a private cubicle and the promise to really use and test his talent. Even better, the office was in San Francisco and the boss was a high profile startup king, Conrad Engstrum. Long hours with a small group of really smart and dedicated people putting together a sure fire integrated technology package that was going to change the world. Only it didn't work and when that became obvious the you know what hit the fan. There was more of course as life can never be that simple. Her name was Sandra Williams.

"Sandra Williams." It hurt Robert just to think her name. They met the afternoon he rented the apartment. April 1, 2014, his thirty-ninth birthday. She was looking at it but had decided she couldn't afford the $3,800 a month rent and was leaving the showing when he walked in. The rental agent was embarrassed at the overlap in the showings but that didn't bother Robert because when you looked at Sandra everything could be forgiven. She stayed as Robert took the tour. Two bedrooms, two baths, kitchen and nice living room with a good view of the Bay. And a parking space. Robert said he would take it and as the agent arranged the paper work Sandra walked over to him and ask if he would like to have a Starbucks with her. The rental agent looked at Robert but said nothing, Robert was a little flustered but said sure and Sandra smiled. Yes to anything. No questions needed to be asked. Not with that smile and with the rest that made up Ms Sandra Williams. He was trying his best to not think about her right now as it just hurt too much. He had other problems to solve and he would address the wounds she had inflicted on him later.

Robert decided he may as well start his day and picked up the box with his kitchen stuff and headed to the elevator and down to the parking garage. He dropped it off in the van and then walked the five blocks to the nearest MacDonald's. Two Egg McMuffins and a cup of coffee. He sat at one of the counters and had company on either side that he was trying to ignore. They seemed to be doing likewise to him and that didn't help his self esteem in the least. It took only a couple of minutes to down the muffins and with the remaining coffee in hand he headed back to the apartment. It wasn't a good start to his day and it wouldn't get any better except for one very interesting thing that did occur that would eventually change his life forever.

Chapter 2

Herbert Robert Johnson was born on April 1, 1975. April Fools Day and his first name was Herbert, which soon became Herbie. How could your parents do such a thing to you? They were good parents, however, and gave him a good childhood and saw to it that he made it through puberty and into adulthood with a very good education and outlook on life. Their life did not go so well as his mother died of cancer just as he was completing college and his father, on a search for some meaning in life, was killed in a climbing accident coming down from the summit on one of those commercial ascents of Mt. Everest ten years ago. Robert had no siblings and no other family relatives so he was pretty much alone. He had a few friends but they could be more accurately described as friendly acquaintances. He tried not to dwell on this but at this moment in his life it did hurt.

As Robert headed back he mused that he really didn't have much to look forward to. There was no way he would try to find another position in the high technology sector, or a start up opportunity, in the near future. Nor would he befriend another beautiful woman, at least until he met one that could compete with Sandra. He had some major scars to heal and it would take some time. He had one period of unemployment before when all he owned was in his car and he was on the road. It had been a good break and there was a feeling of total freedom that was exhilarating. He hoped he could find that spot again. He very much needed to.

He grabbed one of the carts in the garage and headed back to what seemed to be what was left of his life. Not being ready to make the final exit he picked up the eBay parcel off the counter and tried to find a comfortable spot on the floor to sit. It was well packaged and as might be expected with no knife or scissors available he had to tear off the packing by hand. Inside was his "hardly used" iPad3 in it's original box looking hardly used. It showed fully charged at the opening menu so he decided to set it up with his Wi-Fi connection here in the apartment. He had until 5:00 PM to vacate and no place to go so why not do it now.

Two weeks ago trying to balance a third, or maybe it was a fourth, glass of wine while on the balcony browsing the internet, his iPad2 made an unplanned descent to the pavers five stories below. It's remains were in one of the boxes and if the memory could be salvaged he would tend to that later. He quickly did the set up with his ID and Password and was soon into the main page. All the usual Apple Icons were present and he sent an email to himself and that was working. Next he downloaded Google Earth which loaded quickly and showed where his new iPad was located. He would decide what word processor program to get later. He set up his eBay account and the home page started to look like home.

Robert was thinking that maybe that was enough for now when he spotted a rather strange looking Icon in the lower right corner of the screen. It sat there all by itself and had a rather weird symbol in its center. Something like a Trident wrapped in vines, or seaweed, with vaguely shaped human parts exposed. A touch brought up a dark gray screen with a single dark red ENTER button centered with no other information. He better think about this a bit. "What else could possibly go wrong in my life right now?" he said aloud and touched the button.

"You have the chance to visit history as it is happening. Do you have the courage to go there?" was displayed in bold blood red script. Another dark red ENTER button was centered just below. Robert touched it and a fine print agreement page was presented. He scrolled to the bottom and just above an AGREE check box was a warning: "Go back and read the agreement carefully. This is not a game and you, Herbert Robert Johnson, need to fully understand what is being offered and what the penalties are if you do not follow all the rules and instructions in using this program." This was a bit disconcerting to Robert as Herbert had never been used in settings of his on the internet or in any of his private or public nomenclature since his high school days. Nowhere was Herbert used in anything that could be electronically traced in the last twenty plus years. He had even legally changed his name to Robert Johnson and that was even how big brother, federal and state governments, knew him. Robert sat starring at the AGREE box for a few minutes and then he scrolled back up to the top of the AGREEMENTS page and started reading the proverbial fine print. His "Oh My Gods" started almost at the first sentence and continued through the excruciatingly long document.

Chapter 3

It took Robert over half an hour to read through the agreements and he thought of himself as a fast reader. Lots of legalize, but the main points and instructions were clear. What was being offered was incredibly far fetched but none the less so tempting that he would have to consider it. In layman's terms he could pick a time and place to have thirty minutes of an historical person's time and attention. The language would be in his case English and whomever he was speaking to would fully understand and would respond in English. There were some very strict conditions in that his conference would be monitored by five independent minders, each of which could terminate his visit if any part of his discussion could in anyway affect history. This was made abundantly clear by several examples. If this happened his session would immediately be terminated and he would no longer have access to the program. If it was grossly onerous his termination would be such that he may not be able to return to the present day. Since this would all be an out of body experience his self may not be able to totally return to his body with all the associated problems of literally losing part of one's mind. There was a number of requirements. He must be alone and isolated in a safe environment as he would speaking aloud as if his subject was in his presence. He would appear to his subject as himself but clothed in the period's dress. His subject would recognize him as non-threatening and the conversation would be normal. After the conference the subject would have no memory of the meeting but he would retain total recall. His physical self would be defenseless during the conference period and if harm came to it during this time his mind would not be able to return to his body. It was not known what would happen in that case as it hadn't happened yet.

There was much wrapped around this basic revelation and Robert read through the agreement twice more. He decided this would have to be carefully thought about before deciding to go further, but what an opportunity. Several visits were already churning around in his mind. He was somewhat a history buff, as had been his father, and in two of the remaining boxes directly in front of him was his only valuable inheritance, his father's library.

"How about being able to converse with Abraham Lincoln the night before his delivery of the Gettysburg Address while he was putting the finishing touches on his final notes? Would there be a way he could read the speech, and if it read true, convince Lincoln that it was perfect and not to further edit or change a word? Or how about being able to talk to Leonardo da Vinci just before his death about his life, thoughts and be able to tell him of his earned fame in the future?" his mind was racing with the possibilities. Robert started to shake with the anticipation of such adventures. "What did he have to lose? Could this be true or is it just a hoax? Or am I going nuts?" he thought.

He went back to the bottom of the Agreements

page and just below the check box was a questions box. He typed in "I am interested. Can I have a few days to accept?" and touched SEND. Immediately a reply, "FIVE DAYS!" and the screen went blank.

He just sat there looking at the screen lost in thoughts about what this might mean racing through his mind. A ping sounded from the iPad which brought him back to the present. Mail indicated that an email had been delivered to his Inbox. "Beautiful Asian woman looking for a companionship." was displayed. He would have to do some filters on his Email account but now he better hustle as it was time dated 4:39 PM and he had to get moving.

He loaded the cart with the three boxes, suitcases and hanger bag and then toured the apartment again. One last trip to the bathroom and then he placed his apartment key on the counter. He packed his new iPad in the box it had come in and slid it in one of the suitcase pockets, took one last look around and then pushed the cart out the door into the hall, twisted the inside door lock tab and closed the door. His life here was now over and what was to happen next was unknown but he had just been offered an escape. Could he take it if it was real? Did he have the courage? He had five days to decide.

Chapter 4

Robert unloaded the cart into the van and returned it to it's place. Getting in the van he buckled the seat belt and started the engine. "Well, Herbie, where to now?" speaking out loud to himself as Herbie. "My good god," he thought as he backed out of his space and then headed for the exit. His first move was an easy choice because Geary Boulevard was a one-way street so he turned left and headed West. When he reached Park Presidio Boulevard it seemed only natural to turn right and before he had given much more thought on where he was going he was headed North over the Golden Gate Bridge. "Why not? It doesn't make any difference," he thought.

Just as he was mid span on the bridge he had the vision of Sandra all decked out in her new yellow foul-weather gear, looking so damn gorgeous she could be on the cover of Sail magazine, aboard Conrad Engstrum's brand new Tartan 4700 sailboat heading out to sea directly underneath him. "Damn it! Damn it! Damn it! How could that happen right under my nose. How could she do that to me," he yelled at at the windshield. He did know but he was hurting. A blaring horn brought him to his senses and he quickly swerved back into his lane. A little shaken he again thought he would work this out later when he was in the right place and at the right time. Now was not the place or time.

Traffic was not really that bad for a change and with no toll going north on the bridge Robert found himself nearing San Rafael just after six-thirty. His stomach was complaining as he hadn't eaten since his McMuffins early that morning. As he had passed the turn off to Sausalito another flash back of Sandra hit him hard. They would often drive over in his Porsche Carrera S and have dinner at one of the several restaurants that provide the spectacular views of the City on the Bay. A few minutes later he pulled into the restaurant that had the Golden Arches on the outskirts of San Rafael.

It must have been Mom's night out with the children. There was maybe two fathers and a half dozen Hispanic workers, but the other hundred, or so, were harried Moms and their noisy children, none over the age of six. The employees already looked worn out and at least two them were on the clean up crew mopping up spilled drinks and scooping up dropped french fries. Another flash memory of Sandra sitting across from him at a window table for two taking a first sip of wine admiring the view while he admired her.

"Hey, what do you want?" a raspy, accented voice brought him back.

Robert ordered a hamburger, fries and coke to go and wished he had gone through the drive through. He ate in the van and tried to think of his next move. It was starting to get dark and he was starting to fade. There was a nice little State Park, Samuel P. Taylor, a few miles from where he was so he decided he would drive up there and sleep in the van. It was a twenty minute drive, or should have been without the one missed turn, but he arrived at the gate house just after dark. It was closed and "Pay In The Morning" was in the window. Robert drove slowly into the campground and it was sparsely occupied. He found a space away from other campers and pulled in. A quick trip to the restrooms found them clean and adequate. Back in the van he opened the box he had packed with his sheets, a blanket and a small pillow. The air mattress was given several more puffs, placed in the mid-line in the back and made up with his head to the rear and his feet and legs between the rear seats. He took everything out of his pockets and would sleep in his clothes. The minute his head hit the pillow he was wide awake.

Robert would have been staring at the roof of the van but it was totally dark outside and he couldn't see it. Even worse was that he could smell Sandra's fragrance. He had washed the sheets and pillow case after she had left and had only kept the one pillow. It was still there and must be in the blanket. His depression deepened even further. "How could she have done this?" he thought for the hundredth time. He knew. She had spelled it out in her "Dear Robert" letter but he just didn't understand how she could think that way. He could understand the logic, but to do it this way was what hurt him the most.

The letter was printed out and he could see in it's composition that Sandra had spent time and thought in trying to let him down as gently as possible. She wrote of her family which she never, or at least very rarely, had spoken about. It wasn't a happy childhood. Her parents divorced early in their marriage and her father had for all intensive purposes disappeared. Her mother tried early on to provide for her and her older brother. Things rapidly went down hill as alcohol took her mother's youth and health away, and eventually her life. Her brother had joined the Army at 18 and was killed in a freak training accident. She had ended up in several different foster parent situations and managed to get through high school and one year of college relatively unscathed. She then took off on her own from what could hardly be thought of as home.

She came to an understanding on what she had to do to survive. Knowing that she was smart enough, and attractive, she could position herself into situations that would result in employments that would normally require a college degree. It sometimes meant taking a risk but had always been successful.

She wanted Robert to try to understand that was what had happened when they met at the apartment showing. She was almost broke and her new job at the bank payed well but not good enough to live in San Francisco. She couldn't even afford to pay half the rent of an apartment there. The two bedrooms and two bathrooms was good enough and he looked like a really nice guy. She smiled a smile that had worked before and it worked again.

Sandra wrote that she liked him and was as close to loving him as she thought she was capable of loving anyone. Then Engstrum Technologies came more into their lives. As the months progressed she thought that he was the one she had been hoping to someday find. It was then that she felt, for the first time, that maybe totally loving someone was possible.

Over the next few months she had a number of social contacts with Conrad at the various functions that they attended together but nothing more. She liked Conrad as a friend and found him easy to talk to. He had told her a number of times how much he liked him and what a key employee he was. She thought Conrad was genuine.

Two weeks ago with the news of the closing down of Engstrum Technologies she had to make a choice. The life she was hoping to live with him was in jeopardy. She acknowledged maybe having looked into his financial assets enough to know where this was going to go. She had a choice to make and wanted him to understand how hard it was for her to make it. She knew of Conrad's plans with his new sailboat and also knew he had taken care of himself when he formed the company. He needed a shipmate and if that was something she wanted try they could make a trial run to Anacortes, Washington. If that worked out he wanted to sail around the world and if she wanted to, she could go with him.

Sandra ended with that she would always love him, as least as much as she could ever love anyone. Everything they had done together was real and she wasn't sure she could ever again be happier than she had been the last year.

The last sentence in her letter was "You probably don't know this. Conrad is gay."

Chapter 5

It was well past midnight before Robert finally fell asleep. Waking he felt a little less depressed but was longing for Sandra to be snuggled up to him. He would live but it was not going to be as he had hoped just a few days before. He had wanted her to be with him in good times, bad times and forever. It was five-thirty as he drove past the park's closed entry gate house feeling guilty not leaving a payment but he had left only a few footprints and flushed the toilet just twice. Outside the gate he turned left heading towards Point Reyes Station. Driving the Porsche on these roads was a lot more fun than wrestling the van around the many bends and curves. With Sandra in the passenger seat laughing and squealing with excitement there was no comparison.

At Point Reyes Station his first stop was to the Bakery for a sticky bun and a coffee. He then ordered a second sticky bun. The next stop was to the gas station as the yellow warning light on the gas gauge had been on since he left the park. The man at the station stepped out of his office and insisted on pumping the gas for Robert. He thought for a moment that he was in Oregon. They struck up a conversation and once past the weather and which way are you heading it turned to how was business.

Robert said he didn't have any at the moment, or even a job, and the gas station guy offered he was in deep trouble with his.

"I can't get any reliable help these days. Been working fourteen hour days, seven days a week," drawling it out in an exhausted voice.

"Is it worth it? What does your wife think?" Robert asked with sympathy.

"The money is OK but I got a bigger problem than that right now. You wouldn't want a job starting tomorrow for two weeks would you? I'll make it worth your while," the gas station guy asked as if was begging for a gift from heaven.

Robert actually thought about this because he had absolutely nothing to do and didn't really have any place to go. "I don't have any place to stay here."

The gas station guy took a second look at Robert and stuck out his hand. "Jerry Gallager. Did I hear you right? Your not putting me on are you?"

"Robert Johnson. Just recently unemployed with no family, girlfriend, or place to live. So what would you be able to do for me if I say I would do it?" was said with a smile and a chuckle.

"Well Robert I can't drum up a family or a girl-friend for you but I can give you a place to live. It isn't big or fancy but it is clean, dry, warm and just two blocks from here."

Robert could see he was not only serious he was almost desperate. He gave Jerry Gallager his credit card and followed him into the office.

They sized each other up with a little more small talk and then Jerry asked "Would you actually consider doing this?"

"Let's go take a look at the house."

Jerry took a key of the key rack behind his counter and gave Robert the directions to the house. "I need to stay here and you can look it over for as long as you want. You will have to pass muster with the little woman of course but that might not be a problem. We have reservations for a eleven day cruise leaving San Francisco Friday and I can't close up the station, even for a day. Our first vacation in almost two years. Planned and paid for three months ago."

Robert mulled over Jerry's problem as he walked the two blocks to the house. Maybe his problems were a lot worse financially but Jerry's easily topped his. He put the key in the door lock and unlocked the door. It was a small house but the first step in showed a nice living area and modern kitchen. The bedroom was more than adequate and had a queen size bed, dresser, side table and small closet. The bathroom was fine.

Robert thought so far so good. There was one more door which appeared to lead to a second bedroom. Robert entered and it was dark so he groped around for a light switch. The lights came on and he saw the walls and ceiling were covered in acoustic tile, or maybe more like sound proofing baffles. Robert just stood and stared. There were no windows and the door on the inside was also covered in the tiles. A sound proof room. A shudder ran through him and he started to feel a bit nauseous. The agreement specified he be alone and isolated in a safe environment. He would be speaking aloud. This room was as if designed for his exact need if he was to proceed with this weird offer on his iPad. "Coincidence. Are you kidding me!" was Robert's immediate thought.

He closed the front door and locked up the nice little house only two blocks from where he would be working the next few weeks. That is if he passed muster with Mrs. Gallager.

When he told Jerry he was interested in taking him up on his offer he was on the phone immediately and Julie would be here to meet him in a few minutes. She was and took a long look at him after the introductions were made. She was an attractive woman and had the presence of someone that maybe should be in a different place. The station's business was picking up and Jerry suggested that the two of them make a visit to the Bakery so they could talk.

Entering the Bakery Robert was greeted with "No way you can eat another sticky bun," and then a friendly hello to Julie. They took one of the small tables and ordered coffees. Julie was a bit suspicious of Robert but seemed to warm up to him in the first few minutes of their conversation. It was also obvious she really wanted, and needed, to go on the cruise.

"You know, if we do this you have our livelihood in your hands and we know nothing about you," was her first serious comment.

"I can understand that perfectly. This is out of the blue for me too. My position with a start-up technology company in San Francisco came to an end as of yesterday. My love left me two days before that and today is my fortieth birthday. It is also April Fools Day. Can you top that?" was Robert's reply.

Julie looked at him for a rather long time and then started laughing. It was a good laugh. "Is this an April

Fool or am I about to be one?"

"No and no." Robert said with a smile.

"Okay. Let's do it," and they walked back to tell Jerry. The sun had just come out from behind the morning overcast that hovers about the coast almost every morning. It wasn't even time for lunch yet.

Chapter 6

Operating a gas station wasn't brain surgery but there was a lot to learn in a short time. Jerry was busy getting everything lined up so there would be no surprises. Robert had worked in gas stations during his high school and college years and was no stranger to auto mechanics and service. He was also a quick learner. By midday on Thursday Jerry and Julie were so satisfied with their new best friend ever that they headed to San Francisco right after lunch. They were staying with friends in the city and could park their car in their garage. It was ten minutes to the dock and the boarding time wasn't until after twelve noon. It would be, and was, stress free.

Robert had already met a half dozen locals and it seemed there were more than the usual number of ladies of various ages coming in to top off their tanks or purchase what ever in the mini-store. He had been able to stock up the kitchen the night before his full time job started and of course moving in only took a few trips from the van. He closed up the station on Thursday and fixed his first dinner at "home" that evening. A walk down to the end of the street let him meet Browser, a giant red colored Labrador retriever. The owner came out and saved him from being bowled over with affection by the big dog.

Donald Connor, a nationally known artist and a very interesting person. He was older than Robert by about two decades but they had a most friendly conversation and "see you later" salutation on parting company.

That evening Robert checked out the Wi-Fi connection and as Jerry had promised he was able to connect and sign in. It was a high speed service. His Inbox was empty and his Junk Mail had a dozen or more pieces accurately placed in Junk. On his home page he quickly decided there was nothing he wanted to look at but in the lower right hand corner was that odd looking icon. It was blinking. Icons don't usually blink so he touched it. "YOU HAVE THREE DAYS LEFT" in blood red script, with a ENTER button below, came up on the screen. Robert wasn't ready yet. Not tonight, not just yet and maybe never. He collapsed the page and exited it.

He thought his situation over. Risking unknown problems when he had committed to Jerry to take care of his business for two weeks was something he had to consider. He also hadn't decided what he would experiment with if he decided to try it out. Abe Lincoln at Gettysburg was his first choice so he would research that in the morning between taking care of customers. The internet was fabulous for gathering this kind of information. Tomorrow he would make a plan and then decide whether or not to execute it.

He wondered where Sandra was and if she was okay. The thought depressed him and he tried to not think about it but that didn't work. He readied for bed, climbed in and covered up. It was a comfortable bed, the room was the right temperature and it was quiet. He couldn't fall asleep and the memory of having her close caused some tears to form. He was lonelier than he had ever been and was hoping he would be able to get over this. Only a few days had past but now all he could think about was the time he had spent with her over the last year.

The day they met was the day he rented the apartment he had just left two days ago. She was with the rental agent and was readying to leave as he walked in the door. The agent excused himself, approached him with the typical agent's smile and started reciting the apartment details. Sandra had gotten to the door then stepped to the side and calmly waited. He had noticed she was attractive but he needed an apartment. This one was within walking distance of his new job, looked promising and it was what he was wanting. In less than five minutes he was signing the lease and making out the check for $9,600. First month, last month and $2000 damage deposit. San Francisco was expensive.

It was then that she just walked up and asked him to join her for a Starbucks. He took a close look and almost all common sense left him. Very close to five foot ten and wearing low heels she stood almost six feet matching his six two very nicely. Light brown hair, with a perfect golden tint, fell past her shoulders, framing about the most beautiful face he had ever seen. The eyes were light brown with tiny flakes of gold matching the tint in her hair. When he said he'd be delighted her smile put the renting of the apartment completely out of his mind. Dressed nicely in tan slacks, jacket and silk blouse with every inch a perfect fit there was nothing that could stop him thinking this was the most beautiful woman he had ever been in the same room with. The walk to Starbucks was equally revealing. Her stride was athletic, graceful, and feminine to the point of being sensual.

Over the coffees standing at a high table Sandra proposed she could afford $1500 a month for a bedroom and sharing the kitchen. She had few possessions, no bad habits and it was to be understood this would be a platonic relationship. She would entertain no men in her room and he could conduct himself in his own self interest with no interference from her if it was within reason.

The platonic part of the agreement lasted only a few days. "God did he miss her," he was thinking as the tears started coming in earnest.

Chapter 7

Robert started his first full day at Jerry's station at the Bakery having what would become his morning ritual, a glass of orange juice, a fresh baked sticky bun and a cup of coffee. On this morning he was the most popular person there as it appeared everyone knew that Julie and Jerry were going to make their cruise and it was because of him. Julie and Jerry were obviously town favorites and he now was a friend of the town. Robert needed some friendship like that right now.

He had decided that his first trip into history, if he went, would be a visit with Abraham Lincoln at Gettysburg on the evening of November 18, 1863. Lincoln had arrived on the train from Washington, along with a number of friends and three members of his cabinet, late that afternoon. David Wills had been the organizer in Gettysburg that put forward the idea of the Soldiers National Cemetery shortly after the epic battle there on July 1, 2 and 3, 1863. The townsfolk had taken it upon themselves to recover and bury the bodies of the soldiers that had fallen and littered the battlefields in it's aftermath. Wills felt they deserved better than that. He also organized and managed the dedication ceremony on November 19, 1863 at which 25,000 would attend. His house was it's headquarters and Lincoln would stay there overnight on the eighteenth. The Wills had a dinner party for thirty-eight people that evening and Lincoln had retired after it to his guest room to work some more on his address before turning in for the night.

Lincoln had arrived somewhat ill and by the time the evening was ending he must have been exhausted. He had prepared most of his address before he arrived and would be doing some of the last editing in his room that night. It was also thought he may have rewritten the second half of it there. This was where Robert wanted to be as to time and place. A chance to be alone with Lincoln and witness his preparations for the next day when he gave the Gettysburg Address which is thought to be one of the greatest speeches ever made. Robert had memorized it in high school civics and could still repeat it almost verbatim, 272 words. Also, his great great grandfather Johnson, at fifteen years old, had attended the Lincoln-Douglas debate in Ottawa, Illinois on August 21, 1858. His great grandfather had heard his father tell his story a number of times and had written it down for the generations that followed. Robert now had the copy his father had kept and wanted to share that story with Lincoln.

It was these thoughts, and some additional research, that was starting to move Robert in the direction to check the agree box and take the next step. He had a couple of things he had to take care of first. He had to work with someone in Point Reyes to look in on him if something went wrong and help out with Jerry's station if he couldn't. He also decided he had to contact Sandra. He just couldn't let her go without trying to make it possible for something to re-unite them in the future. Even just a friendship would be better than never seeing her again. Less than a week had passed and it already seemed like a year.

The twelve hour day flew by. It seemed like half the town stopped by and a surprising number made purchases. The tourist traffic was much heavier than he had anticipated. Robert then thought Jerry was right, he had to be open twelve hours a day, seven days a week. The only other business in town that had traffic like that was the Bakery across the street. Even Browser, with Donald Connor on the other end of the leash, came for a visit. Only after Browser had his head patted, ears pulled and a good back rub did Robert and Donald have a chance to talk. After some pleasantries, and a bit of information Robert was hoping for in that Donald had helped out Jerry a few times at the station, he asked if he might stop over this evening for brief visit. It was set for eight o'clock and Robert began to think that his life might be worth while again.

Chapter 8

Robert ordered a sandwich for his lunch from the Bakery and crossed the street during a lull to pick it up. The soup menu looked good and they would set aside a bowl for him and warm it up for his dinner after he closed up the station. It seemed he was getting a routine established before his first full day was over. It was comfortable here and he was already on a first name basis with the Bakery staff. Point Reyes Station was a nice place with good people.

This was making his coming choice to risk it all, and maybe everything, to visit with Abe Lincoln on the evening of November 18, 1863 more difficult. He planned to discuss with Donald the possibility of him covering Jerry's station if things went badly for him. How he was going to explain what he was thinking of doing he had no idea. He would have to play it by ear.

Robert closed up the station at seven-thirty and was just walking away when a car drove in and then seeing the closed sign headed down the street to the only other gas station in town. He wondered if he would make it before it also closed as this was about when the town started it's evening rest. Only the Bakery was open until nine and then it too turned off the lights. His soup was ready and came with an extra large roll and three patties of butter.

He knocked on Donald's door at eight exactly and a baritone "woof, woof" was loud and clear. The door was opened and Robert did his now demanded greeting to Browser. Donald stood back and grinned. He was a big man, taller than Robert by at least two inches and about forty pounds heavier. The pounds weren't fat and his hands were huge. It was a fine greeting as far Robert was concerned and although the handshake was firm it wasn't what it could have been if he had wanted to put you in your place. A gentle giant came to mind. Donald had a small artist's paint brush in his other big hand and invited Robert into his studio which at one time had probably been the dining room. He had another two additional work spaces in the back for pursuing larger works and doing woodworking.

Robert was taken aback by what was on the easel. It was a very beautiful swan on a rippled pond with cattails and other vegetation in the background. One could almost say it was delicate but it was definitely a beautiful painting. Donald said "I have just a few minutes more on this and then it will be set aside so I can decide if it is finished. Have a seat over there and give me a minute." The big hand holding the small brush made a number of strokes, touching the palette on the stand next to him and then the painting leaving just the suggestion of ripples around the swan. They grew outward as if by magic and in five minutes Donald placed the brush in glass of water, swirled it about, then wiped it gently with a towel. "There! That's enough for now. Let's go to my study."

Robert was still trying to comprehend what he had

just seen. Browser, however, headed in front of them to the study. His giant dog bed was there and he made two turns around in it and went down in a heap, exhaling a loud "huff" while looking at Robert with what could only have been a smile, and then slowly closed his eyes. Donald pointed to a comfortable chair and rested his big frame into a bigger one. This almost giant of a man was painting these exquisite and beautiful paintings. There were photographs of him, and one could assume the woman in many to be his wife, covering the walls. Obviously an outdoors man and hunter having traveled extensively in those pursuits. He waited patiently.

"I don't know how to explain what I need to talk to you about as no matter how I do it it won't make much sense," was Robert's opening line. Donald looked at him and then smiled a patient smile. "I have been through a lot in the last two weeks. March twentieth I found out that the start up company I had joined a year ago was folding up. I was out of a high paying and interesting job, my stock options were worthless, and there would be no severance pay. My cost of living in San Francisco was much too expensive to continue. I gave up my apartment, my leased Porsche, my leased furniture. My live in love of my life left me for the chance to sail around the world with my ex-boss and founder of the company, who by the way is gay, on the twenty-eighth and I was homeless on the thirty-first. It has been a rough two weeks."

Donald wasn't smiling any more and just said "Jiminy Crickets! That's one sad story. Glad it didn't happen to me. What company was that?"

"Engstrum Technologies."

"Your kidding me. There was article in the Wall

Street Journal about a week ago about that. Sounded like Engstrum took off with a lot of money, all legal I guess, but he sure left the employees with nothing and I assume the venture capitalists are in a bad mood." Then Donald asked "How did you end up here?"

Robert filled him in with the details right up to knocking on his door just now. He then continued with what had really hurt the most was losing Sandra.

"I'll give you some advice on that, don't give up completely on her. Women, especially beautiful ones, some times panic when their plans are disrupted and love sometimes takes a backseat. A sailboat ride around the world is not as romantic as it sounds. I have done it and it is really hard on a person unless they like to be miserable most of the time. It does have it's moments but it doesn't sound to me like she would be one to be able to take the beating. Give her a little time and see what happens. You being broke and running a gas station might not look so bad after a few stormy days at sea." Donald took a deep breath then asked "What is it that I can help you out on?"

Chapter 9

Robert was in a quandary on how to approach him as he was just old enough to be his father but just a bit too old to be his older brother. He didn't know much of his background but he was established as being one of the best water colorists of his genre in the country and had been for some time. He also had been a resident in Point Reyes for years and lived in the same home the whole time. There was much to like about him and Robert did just that. He decided to approach him head on and let the chips fall where they may.

"Donald, I am going to treat you as a old and valued friend that will trust me in not being a nut case. You should know I have a Computer Science degree from MIT and a masters degree in Business from Stanford. I pride myself with the ability to reason and I detect in you a similar trait. What I am about to tell you is totally, however, irrational. So irrational it embarrasses me to tell anyone." Robert paused and looked at Donald for a reaction. There was none which he decided was the correct one.

"You know I have been under stress the last two weeks and what I am going to tell you about happened in the last couple of hours before I had to exit my apartment, just four days ago. I had set up my new, hardly used, iPad

I had bought on auction on eBay. I noticed a strange Icon all by itself in the lower right corner of the screen and touched it." Donald leaned forward and Robert could tell he was interested and not put off with his lead up to what he trying explain.

"On a gray screen, in dark blood red script, was 'You have the chance to visit history as it is happening. Do you have the courage to go there?' with a enter tab centered underneath. I touched it and an agreement page came up and I scrolled to the bottom without reading it." Robert paused again and Donald's expression changed only slightly, showing curiosity but not disbelief. Encouraged he continued, "There was an agree box to be checked but it was here I had to stop. Just above it was 'Go back and read the agreement carefully. This not a game and you, Herbert Robert Johnson, need to fully understand what is being offered and what the penalties are if you do not follow all the rules and instructions in using this program.' Donald nobody, including me, has used my first name Herbert in over twenty years. I legally changed it to Robert Johnson. Even my name on Federal and State records is Robert Johnson."

Robert leaned back in his chair and Donald didn't hesitate to enter the conversation.

"That's quite a story. You have piqued my interest and I can accept your belief that it is not a hoax. That is what I would have thought but having your name like that makes it a challenge to just blow it off. I take it the agreement was an interesting read."

Robert was surprised and relieved. He now knew his first impression of Donald had been correct and he had someone with whom he could talk. Relief was almost over whelming and he started to choke up a bit. He needed help and to have someone right now was important.

He decided to change the subject just a bit. "I will get to the details in a minute, but I have a question for you. It's about Jerry's little house. I never got around to ask him about the sound proof room. Looks like a converted bedroom and that it was installed just recently. Did you see it put in or know anything about it?"

Donald looked surprised at the question, thought about it for a moment, then answered. "I was wondering about that. A few days ago an unmarked white utility van showed up and started unloading a number of medium sized boxes and putting them inside. I was taking Browser on his daily walk and was gone about an hour. When I came back the van was gone. Didn't think anything about it as I just assumed Jerry was having some stuff he had ordered delivered. Didn't bother me at the time but now I remember thinking that the boxes couldn't have been very heavy as the guys were toting them in two at at a time."

Robert had that same feeling he had when he first saw the room the day before yesterday. Frightened. "Donald, part of the Agreement was to find a place where I could be alone, isolated and safe. I would be speaking aloud as if my subject would be in my physical presence but I would actually be at the location of the event speaking to him, or her, or them. There would be no audible responses. A sound proof room in a small private house would be perfect."

Donald then responded, "Coincidence! No way man! You got to be kidding!" His response lifted Robert spirits even more. He now knew he could talk freely to him and seek his advice and help.

Just then the lady in the photographs on the wall stuck her head in and greeted them both. She had been in the City and her meetings had lasted longer than expected, she was tired and would just say Hi. A "Pleased to meet you," to Robert was his introduction to Diane Connor. She did add it was so good of him to take over for Jerry and Julie as they really needed a break from home for a bit.

After Diane hurried out Robert filled in the rest of his story including the blinking Icon and the "you have three days left" which meant Sunday evening. He added he didn't know what would happen when he checked the agree box and touched enter. Something was going on here and he needed some help.

"What do think?"

"I am glad it is not me," was Donald's quick response.

Chapter 10

The second full day at the station had ended like the first except Saturday seemed to be much busier than Friday. Jerry had an accountant, namely Julie, that would go through the receipts and tapes so for Robert's period he just put everything in a business storage box and the cash in the floor safe. He was to make deposits in even dollar amounts every three days. That he could do and hoped all would sort out correctly when they got back.

When he had headed to the small house after the meeting with Donald he had decided to email Sandra and wait one more day before checking the AGREE box and touching ENTER. Donald agreed with him that he should take the next step if just for curiosity's sake, both hoping that curiosity would not kill the cat.

As soon as the home page came up the strange Icon was blinking and Robert decided to let it blink. He went to Email and touched New and entered Sandra's address from the contact list. He then just stared at the blinking cursor for a few minutes trying to compose in his mind what to write. "Why is this so hard to do. Make it short and sweet no matter how much you want to say to her. Don't make it worse," talking out loud to himself and glad he was alone.

He typed "Sandra, I hope you are OK and I miss you. If you need anything I am here for you. Robert". He read it over three times and knew it was probably all he should write. A broken heart and wanting her back so badly it hurt him even more than how she had decided to end their relationship. He hoped that Donald's advice might turn out to be correct and there was a chance that she would be part of his life again. He touched Send and it was gone.

The home screen came back and the Icon on the lower right hand corner was blinking what seemed to Robert to be even faster than before. He was so depressed he touched it and YOU HAVE ONE DAY LEFT came up and he touched ENTER, checked the AGREE box and then ENTER. The gray screen had centered a white box headed by INFORMATION in black Times New Roman and where on the left edge of the box, one above the other and separated with lines forming smaller boxes, were WHEN, WHERE, and WHY. Robert filled in "November 18, 1863", "Abraham Lincoln's bedroom, David Wills house, Gettysburg, Pennsylvania, USA", and "To visit Lincoln as he did his final editing of The Gettysburg Address. Hopefully to find out if it was as now thought to have been delivered and to assure him it was perfect as written. If time permitted telling him the story about my great great grandfather being at the Lincoln-Douglas debate in Ottawa, Illinois August 21, 1858. He would not identify who he was."

Another button appeared but this time a not threatening SUBMIT. Robert did not hesitate and touched it. The box with his answers disappeared immediately and "Thank you Robert Johnson. Your request will be reviewed and an answer will be sent within twenty-four hours with further instructions if accepted." The screen went blank. Robert stared at it for about an hour. He thought okay and then all he could visualize was Sandra walking with him on a beach. She was smiling. "Please," was his only thought.

Chapter 11

Sunday was like Saturday but even busier as the Bay Area crowd did their good weather driving excursions. Robert remembered the several he had made, the best with Sandra next to him, as the Porsche made the driving a pleasure. The day went by and Jerry's station was doing so well he was starting to worry about running short of gas and everything in the store. Gas stations had changed quite a bit in the twenty years since he was last an attendant. It was starting to change then but it was now almost like the gas was the secondary purpose for the business. It appeared the big earners were giant soft drinks and potato chips. Jerry had arranged for his suppliers to check in more often and restock when necessary which took most of the pressure off him.

Robert followed the previous day's routine and was glad when seven-thirty arrived. It was eight-fifteen, however, before he got closed. This night it was the Bakery's stew for dinner and he finished just as they were trying to close. They would be there a little longer as several other customers seemed to be struggling to finish up. It was a nice place and tough to leave if you were now having to drive back to the City.

When Robert stepped into the little house, just two

blocks away from work, a feeling of loneliness swept over him that he was afraid would become permanent. He opened up his iPad and went directly to Mail. His Inbox was empty and the gloom became almost unbearable. It was good he had this day job to keep his mind off his problems. "Buck up, you wimp," he muttered to himself.

He went back to the Home Page and looked at the bottom right of the screen and there was no strange looking Icon there. "Well, maybe it is over. Is it over?" he said out loud with the accent on the question.

"Good evening Robert," scrolled across the middle of the screen in clean black print. Directly underneath, centered, was ENTER. He was startled as much of the fright factor in the earlier communications was not there anymore. He touched ENTER.

There was a letter with the salutation and content very simply stating "Dear Mr. Robert Johnson, Your request has been reviewed by the board and we have decided unanimously to accept it. We will be in contact within seven days with instructions on how we will proceed. You can plan on making this first visit two weeks from today at approximately this same time. We are looking forward to working with you. You may wish to start thinking about who and where you may want to visit next as we are confident you will want to continue." There was no signature, letter head, or valediction.

The next two days were uneventful for Robert at the gas station. Jerry's suppliers arrived at various times on Monday and Tuesday, took inventories, restocked the shelves, and told him that business was up ten percent and Jerry would be happy. The big gas truck came on Tuesday afternoon and filled the three underground tanks. The driver said Jerry was having a good two weeks and he might have to make a special delivery before the next one scheduled. He showed Robert how to measure with the tank's dip stick. He suggested a week hence and wrote down the numbers that were expected. If there was less than that they would make an additional delivery to make sure he didn't run out. It seems all was going very good at Robert's new place of employment.

Donald had stopped by on Monday afternoon with Browser leading the way and it was now for sure that he had taken a real liking to Robert. A full head pat, ear pull and a thorough back rub was required before any conversation was allowed between the men. It almost seemed Donald enjoyed this as much as Browser did. The reason for the visit was to invite Robert for dinner at eight the next evening, which was accepted with much appreciation.

Tuesday was similar to Monday, without any interruptions other than the gas delivery, and Robert was able to close the station on time and with a quick stop at the little house he changed clothes, brushed his teeth, washed his hands and face, and combed his hair. He then judged that most of the station's odors were taken care of. He still had 5 minutes so he opened his iPad and checked for mail. There wasn't any in the Inbox and none from Sandra. He looked in Junk Mail and among about six or seven was one that seemed unusual as there was no subject, just his name Robert Johnson. He touched the bar and the message was "Mr. Robert Johnson, you will receive a small package delivered by a private Currier tomorrow at the station. It will have a return address from LaSalle Street, Chicago, IL and addressed to you by name only. Open this when you are alone. Explanation and instructions will be inside as will be several small electronic gadgets. Secure the electronics in a safe place and at your leisure read the written material. You will be contacted Sunday night at exactly eight o'clock via the internet. You may continue discussing the program with Donald Connor. There are and will be no liability to him knowing about your involvement with us and in fact we would like him to know about the risks you maybe exposed to and to handle your affairs if any thing unforeseen happens. We look forward to working with you."

He was now five minutes late and rushed the half block to the Connor's.

Chapter 12

Robert knocked on the door and it was opened by Diane who welcomed him with a smile and please come in. He was taking his first step across the threshold when he heard the baritone woof-woof and saw the big head of Browser coming down the hall at almost full speed from Donald's den. A big voice yelled out "Get out of the way Diane! Now!" What happened next happened fast but to Robert it was almost in slow motion. Browser was up to full speed crossing the small living room and then tried to hit the brakes with all four paws on a small entry rug in unison. Robert jumped straight up, spreading his legs, and luckily Browser lowered his head as he and the rug slid out over the door landing onto the porch. Another woof-woof and he got turned around and came back to Robert with a smile and his big tail whipping back and forth. It was time for Robert's greeting and he provided it with gusto. "What have you done to my dog?" Donald yelled and then the laughter began. For a few minutes Robert was genuinely happy. It had been some time since he had felt this way and he needed it badly.

Diane had jumped safely out the way and had the best view. Her laughter was wholehearted and filled the room. When things calmed down she said, "Dinner will be in fifteen minutes so why don't you two go back to the den and take the big oaf with you."

They had a few minutes and Robert told Donald about the email and that it had mentioned him by name.

"How did they know you had talked to me about this thing? You didn't tell them about me did you?"

"No. Not a word. But they encouraged me to let you be part of it just in case something went wrong. I don't exactly know what that means but in the agreement there is a part that if I do anything, and they stress anything, that could change the future I may be stuck there mentally and my myself would remain here," Robert replied.

Donald took a second long look at Robert and said, "I think we will have to spend some time discussing this."

"I am receiving a small box tomorrow with some instructions and small electronic gadgets. They will contact me on Sunday night at eight o'clock. Let's get together after that. I want your help and advice but only if there is no risk to you"

Another long look came Robert's way and then in an almost whisper Donald said, "Okay."

"Dinner is ready! You two get out here before it gets cold." There was no delay from the boys but Browser seemed perfectly content in his dog bed and only opened one eye as they left the room.

It was a great meal. The best Robert had eaten in years. Even better than at any of the fine restaurants he had taken Sandra to in San Francisco. Pheasant on a bed of wild rice and on the side were carrots and spinach and a selection of wild mushrooms. Donald and Diane had hunted the pheasants, grown the carrots and spinach, and the wild mushrooms they had gathered. The tastes were fantastic. Robert's plate was cleaned completely. He noticed that each plate was different and asked Diane, "I see the plates are all different and look like antiques. Does this have a story?"

She smiled. "How nice of you to notice. These, and most of the china I use, have been handed down through the generations. Your plate was one from my grandmother's wedding set. Donald's is another generation older from the same side of the family, and mine traveled from Pennsylvania to Illinois on a covered wagon in 1851 and then by train, with a few stops along the way, to California. I have one more plate, a cup, and one small bowl left in that set."

"What a nice story. I feel honored that you would serve me on one of your collection." Robert was touched. He had lucked out coming to Point Reyes. That thought suddenly disappeared when he remembered the sound proof room a half block from where he sat. Diane said she would clean up if you boys want to talk a bit.

Donald looked at Robert. "Lets just sit here a few minutes. I have a suggestion for you which you might like. Do you know what AIS is, and more importantly Satellite AIS?"

"It sounds familiar but I can't place it."

"AIS is Automatic Identification System and Satellite AIS is the same type using satellites for location determination. Just like your car's navigation GPS except in reverse. There are several companies that provide ship positions world wide. Not only big ship positions but recreational vessels, such as sailboats. Conrad Engstrum's sailboat has a S-AIS. Some tracking services are even free and with the vessels name, identified by the owner's name or boat make and length, you can follow it world wide live as long as the transmitter is turned on. The only reason he would have installed this system is for safety and security. He would have it on anytime he is out to sea. Many boaters leave it on while they are in port and even when they plan being away for an extended period of time. It is always nice to know where your boat is even when you are not on it." Donald gave Robert a knowing look.

"I think I was just served dessert," was Robert's answer to Donald look. "I can find out the boats name easy enough and I know the make and length. I think I have something to do tonight before I fall asleep."

"Robert, you can get to sleep even sooner." Donald handed him a three by five card with a name, a few numbers and the website of a vessel location service. "Sandra is in Fort Bragg right now. Leave her alone for now. She will let you know when it is time."

Chapter 13

When Robert got back to the little house he didn't feel quite as lonely as the last time he had entered it just a few hours earlier. He now felt secure that he had some good friends that he could turn to when he needed help or company. He looked at the card Donald had given him and went on-line and brought up the website on his iPad. The boat's name was *Du-eT*. A play on words he didn't understand but it didn't bother him. Tartan 4700 was next and then Conrad Engstrum, owner. A search resulted in a chart like map with a small boat shaped marker. The latitude and longitude co-ordinates were highlighted and Ft. Bragg, California was spelled out as was the Marina's name. The boat was pointed south east into the slip. That was were Sandra was now. It gave him comfort but Donald was right, he had to be patient and let this work it self out. He clicked on a favorite Save Icon and he could now with just a click be able to know her location. It gave some comfort but didn't quell his unhappiness. Very tired and not wanting to think anymore he went to bed. Sleep came quickly for a change and he made it through the entire night without waking.

His day at the station started out as normal after his downing the exceptionally good sticky bun at the Bakery.

At exactly eleven o,clock a car pulled into the outside gas lane and a very ordinary looking young man approached the office. He asked for Robert Johnson and before Robert could even say that was he, the man asked to see some identification. Robert presented his drivers license and received in return a six by nine inches padded envelope and was bid good day by the youngster as he returned to his car. Robert looked at the envelope addressed simply Mr. Robert Johnson with a return address of LaSalle Street, Chicago, Illinois. He looked up and the car was gone. He could not remember what kind of car it was, not even the color, and had no idea of what the courier looked like or even how tall he was. Robert thought of the popular PGA slogan,"These guys are good."

The day continued along as had the previous one. He had brought his iPad with him and clicked on the vessel location Icon shortly after opening up the station. The small boat marker was out to sea and was pointing North. It was already past Westport so they must have made an early start. Sailboats don't travel very fast even when under power. Eight miles an hour was about average. Robert thought he should find a chart book or cruising guide to follow their progress. Then he thought maybe he shouldn't. It did seem like spying but he did want to know where she was so he would decide about that later.

Soup was on the menu that evening at the Bakery and one of the staff brought him a big bowl and some freshly baked bread along with extra butter and a small dish filled with which could only be homemade strawberry jam. He had a small soft leather case that carried his iPad and the padded envelop just fitted in the outside pocket. Feeling very comfortably fed he decided a walk around the side of town opposite his little house would be just right and in about twenty blocks of walking he was back where he had started. Three blocks later he was home. The only thing missing was a greeting from Browser. Whatever the attraction was with that dog Robert had started to treasure it. He was pretty sure Donald was not enthused because if Browser was supposed to be a hunting dog that was no way to act. The thought brought a smile to his face. Maybe Browser knew how badly he needed some unconditional love right now.

Robert sat down at the small table that served as the dining table with room for two. He slid the padded envelop from his iPad case and turned it over in his hands. It was so light that he thought it might be empty. He used a small paring knife to slice it open on the sealed end and pulled out several standard letter size sheets of paper folded in half and a small box about two by four inches and one half inch thick. The box was in a tight fitting clear plastic zip lock bag. Unfolding the papers found them well covered with neatly typed information and instruction. The first page outlined information on the contents of the pouch.

The first line was to carefully store the box in a secure, dry and safe place in the house and other than examining the contents do not try to use or experiment with any of them. Robert found a clean kitchen towel and spread it on the table. Opening the zip lock he carefully slid out the box, removed several small discs of tape and took off the lid. Inside were two items that looked like very small hearing aids. One had a red dot and the other a green one. Port and starboard, left and right surmised Robert. Each had a slender skin colored tab which looked like it was to be used to extract the device with tweezers as there would be no way to reach them with fingers if inserted fully in. Their small size was surprising for such devices. Along the side of the box were the plastic tweezers.

Robert set the ear devices to one side and picked another item out of the box. It was much larger than the ear pieces but still small for any kind of transmitter which was what he deduced he was looking at. It weighed almost nothing but was an odd shape with one side having what looked like a spiral coil of small wire embedded in the plastic body case. It was maybe one and a half inches in diameter but not really a disk. The last item looked very much like a zippo lighter, about a three inch long cylinder, and the only item that was metallic. Robert turned these over several times each and then put everything back in the box in their indents in the foam pad, slid the box back in the bag and zipped it closed. What ever they were they were small devices and he was curious as to their function. He would have to find a good place to hide them.

The second page stated that this Sunday evening at 8:00 PM he was to be in the sound proof room and instructions would be sent to him online. He was to be prepared with the devices on the table and his iPad connected to the internet. The session would take one hour and a practice run would be made to make sure everything was working. There would be no risk for him and the devices would pose no problems. The ear pieces were to be placed in his ears, red left and green right. The smaller of the remaining two devices, which was a transmitter, receiver and microphone could be placed anywhere near his person. The cylinder could placed anywhere in the room or left in the box. It was a battery charger.

The last instruction was that he should be seated comfortably facing his iPad as part of his preparation required was essentially hypnosis. He would have to remain in that position for as much as one hour, but it should be less than that. Again it was repeated that on this exercise there was no danger to him. Robert thought, "Yea, sure! Where have I heard that before."

The last sheet of paper had nothing written, just an arrangement of concentric circles in various line thickness and color and an array of similar looking horizontal and vertical lines. He stared at them a minute or two and began to feel a tinge of light headness. He could guess what it might be used for.

Chapter 14

The next two days went without any change in pace. Breakfast at the Bakery was now just placed in front of him when he sat down at the community table. Hello's and Hi's were exchanged as was small talk. Robert had been adopted by the locals and he was now sure that if he didn't show up by seven-thirty at the Bakery an all points bulletin would be sent out. It had been years since he had the feeling of belonging somewhere. He liked it.

That afternoon Browser stopped by for a visit and as usual Donald was on the other end of the leash. After the required greeting Donald proposed it would be a good evening for him to visit the little house and straighten out some things on Robert's first experiment with his visit to the past. Eight o'clock was good as the next evening was to be the first online contact.

Browser was well behaved when Robert opened the door but still required some special attention before they could enter. Then a strange thing happened as he started the rounds of sniffing all the new smells in the little house. When he reached the door to the sound proofed room the hairs on his back stood up, he lowered his head, his eyes narrowed and he let out a most menacing growl.

Robert looked at Donald and quickly said, "That

doesn't look promising."

"Browser doesn't like something in there. Dogs know when something not right. Lets go outside on the porch and talk," was Donald's suggestion. There were two chairs on the porch and it was a nice evening so Robert grabbed a sweater and the three of them got comfortable. Browser calmed as soon as they left the house but there was no doubt he hadn't liked what was on the other side of that door. It sent a shiver down Robert's spine.

The two men looked at each other and both understood what had just happened. It was going to make the project more difficult to talk about from both points of view. Robert started by describing the delivery of the package, it's contents and the instructions. He told Donald all the details and what he was thinking would happen Sunday night. Donald was very cautious in his response and said, "I wouldn't go there if it was me but you are not me. I have a lot to lose and wouldn't risk it. What's your thinking?"

Robert took a long time before answering but Donald was patient and Browser had fallen asleep with one of his big paws on his foot. Finally he started. "Donald, common sense says no, don't go there. If I thought that my life was now going to be everything I wanted it to be I wouldn't go there. But right now I have little to lose and just the idea that this might be legitimate makes me want to the take this first step. So I am going to do it."

They sat there for several minutes not saying anything. Browser started to jerk his legs a bit in a running motion, then stretched and let out a yawn and relaxed back down. Donald asked "What do you want me to do?"

"They wrote about it taking about one hour starting

at eight. Could you come over about nine-thirty and check on me. I have an extra key and will have locked the door. Jerry and Julie will still be one day from returning and if I don't make it back, mentally, can you work out something to cover the station? I am not sure what you can do about me if need be but there should be some kind of public assistance that can take care of a crazy person."

Donald gave Robert another long look and then came back with, "I can certainly understand you wanting to go there. If I was in your shoes I would do it too. I will take care of whatever needs to be done so don't worry about that."

"I don't deserve to have a friend as good as you. You understand this. Most would just tell me you're crazy and walk away. Thanks."

Again the two sat in silence for several minutes then Robert excused himself and asked Donald to wait just a moment and went in the house. He came back with a manila envelope. "This is for you to keep for me. It has some value so keep it safe. If I don't come back capable of taking care of myself just follow the instructions. Should be self explanatory."

Donald stood up and they shook hands. Robert gave him the extra key and Browser got untangled from between their legs, looked around the porch and then up at Robert. He had the saddest look you have ever seen on a dog.

Robert thought, "Oh oh."

Chapter 15

Robert was in the sound proof room sitting in front of his iPad which was propped up at a good angle for viewing. It was on and the clock on the home page was showing 7:48 PM and Sunday April 12, 2015 was displayed. He had the small box open with the gadgets within reach. His nerves were starting to jangle and the clock made it to the next minute. He had no idea what was to happen next. Another minute passed.

It had been the busiest day yet at the station. Almost non-stop from ten-thirty on. The Bakery delivered his sandwich which he managed to get down between servicing a dozen customers. He hadn't had time to even think about what was to take place when he got seated in his current position staring at the small iPad screen. Point Reyes Station was in all it's glory as mid-April was when the weather was best until fall. The old adage that "The coldest winter I ever spent was July in San Francisco," was a truism and this day was about as good as it could get. It seemed half the City had come to visit.

He did get closed on time and the Bakery came through again with dinner. Donald stopped by as he was closing up but Browser was not leading this time. He walked up to Robert and just leaned against his thigh and looked up with those sad eyes. A shudder of dread welded up in Robert. "He knows, doesn't he?' Robert asked Donald.

"He's been like this all day. You damn well come out of this okay or I am going to kick your sorry ass up and down Main Street," had been Donald's rejoinder.

7:58 PM showed on the clock. Then 7:59 PM. Then 8:00 PM.

"Hello Mr. Johnson," made Robert almost fall off his chair. He hadn't made any preparation for sound and the best he could answer was a feeble, "Yes."

"Don't be alarmed. We have complete control of your iPad and will be using it for most of our communications. Is this satisfactory for you?" The voice was calm, neutral, non-threatening.

"Yes. Yes that is fine with me."

"Good. Let's get started. So far everything has gone very well. We, myself and our staff, are more than pleased with you. You are an ideal subject for our project. I will try to answer your question as best and as clearly as I can. Some will not be answered so I will start with those that can be. You may address me as John."

"You have my attention, John."

"As you are probably the best candidate we have had so far we are really looking forward to your participation. You are already aware that we are able to work with you to a great extent without your knowledge or participation so we hope you can accept what has occurred so far without our need to explain how it was accomplished. Is that okay with you?'

"Yes," Robert answered.

"Good. What we are trying to perfect is placing a

person in a position as a witness to a historic time to better understand what actually happened. In no way do we wish to change anything in the past. That is mandatory. In fact we think we have made this requirement fool proof. It should be obvious to you why that is mandatory. You do understand this?"

"Yes."

"Good. Now what you can expect is that you will be transported to a time and place in thought only. Your being will remain in your present position during your travel back in time. This is where our technology becomes less comprehensible and it will not be explained to you in any detail. What you will encounter is consciousness of being in the time and place and you will be able to communicate in speech only. The real magnificence is that your subject, or subjects, will be able to respond in your language and will observe you as you look but in attire compatible with the time. A neat trick, don't you think?"

Robert smiled and repeated another, "Yes."

"Mr. Johnson, you don't disappoint. There will be no physical contact. None. Physically you are not there. This is probably the most difficult part in the participation and is also the most difficult part in the technology to accomplish. We will not be able to answer any questions on this part of our program. You will have total recall of your visit and your subject, or subjects, will have absolutely no recall. We will of course have recorded the complete audio portion but there will be no video. Your memories will be your property and you may use them as you wish. Do you wish to continue?"

"Yes."

"Good. Place the ear device with the red dot in left

ear and green one in right. Place the small disc next to your iPad. You should be hearing my voice through the ear devices and respond if this is so."

Robert said "Loud and clear, John."

"Roger that as we used to say," was the immediate response. "We will now converse with our devices. I trust they are working?"

"Okay," Robert said to the empty room.

"Good. We are ready for your first visit to the past. We have picked out something we think you will enjoy. Please understand you only have thirty minutes maximum with this equiPMent and on this first trip you will have just ten minutes. There is no danger to you or your subjects. Are you ready?"

"Yes," was Robert's immediate answer.

Chapter 16

Robert glanced at the iPad screen. 8:12 PM. Then the screen filled with the concentric circles and lines that looked like the ones on the third page of the papers that came in the envelope. John's voice came over the ear plugs clear, soft and emotionless. "You can see on your iPad screen a pattern. It is used to aid in hypnotizing you. This is the first step and once accomplished your next clear vision will be at the time and location that has been chosen. Again, remember you will have no physical presence there although to the subjects you will appear as if you are real. You should find yourself comfortable almost immediately so just relax and carry on. There will be one beep when your time is almost done, then three fast ones when only thirty seconds remain. You will awaken back in the present in the same position you are now in and will have total recall of your visit. Our hypnosis always works and is fast. Are you ready?"

"Yes," said Robert with no hesitation and there was an immediate response by another voice. Before he could even think this wouldn't work the circles and lines on the iPad screen merged in a slow rotation and he found himself standing on a green lawn with a number of trees in Fall foliage about. There was a young man, maybe just a boy, about fifteen feet away holding a camera pointing his way. The boy said "smile" and the big camera clicked and whirred the next frame of film into place. A man's familiar voice right next to Robert said, "Thank you," and Robert turned his way. It was his father.

"Dad?" muttered Robert in a quiet voice as he took a second look. In the background was the MIT Great Dome atop the Maclaurin Building. He was in Killian Court and his father had just retrieved his camera and turning back towards Robert said "That should be a good picture of the three of us here in the Center of the Universe. Don't you think, Jane?" Robert spun in the other direction and blurted out, "Mom?"

"You okay Robert?" his mother's cheerful voice rang out. "Did you just wake up to where you are? Hey Danny, Robert just woke up. Our MIT freshman is ready to start college now that he is awake."

They were both laughing and smiling. His mother was young and beautiful. Her voice clear and lovely. His Dad handsome with that great smile he always wore. Robert tried his best to smile and said, "Wow, how did I get here. What a great place."

"You earned it, Son. You earned it. It's great, just great. Let's continue the tour."

They went on. The big building under the dome, the science and engineering buildings and then a trip to his dorm room. Robert had now adjusted and the conversation was just as it had been that time in the Fall of 1994. Full of happy talk and excitement about the future. Robert knew what the future held but this was now and he didn't want anything to be different than it had been then. It was so much more important now, so much more. What a gift to be able as an adult to live this day again. His parents so proud and happy and he, this time, so glad he could see them that way again.

The conversation was fast and constant and his mother remarked to his father, "You know I think MIT is already having an effect on our boy. He seems to know where he is and is speaking in complete sentences."

"Will wonders never cease."

Robert was happy to see them this way. Then he heard the first beep.

They continued touring the dorm and then went outside on the grounds. More classmates were arriving with their families. His father took him aside and in a more serious tone started a different conversation, one Robert had not thought about in a long time.

"Robert, I entered Cal Berkeley in 1964. The Viet Nam war was escalating, the Hippy movement was under-way and a thing called the Free Speech Movement hit the big time. A bunch of radical leftist, even Communist lean-ing, students and graduate student teachers were involved. They thought they knew everything. There was an old Polish longshoreman philosopher in San Francisco named Eric Hoffer who commented 'Deez kids, day douh noh nauthing,' and he was right. Don't get involved with peo-ple like these. They are idealists and idealists have an un-canny way of making everyone around them unhappy. You are here to learn. Learn it well and it will serve you well. Do us proud here as you have done so far. We will always be here for you."

Robert could say nothing for a moment without starting to cry as he knew their future. Fortunately his mother called out that it was time for them to head home to beat the traffic. Three beeps broke through his consciousness as he walked them towards their car and waved goodbye.

The next thing he knew he was back in his chair in front of his iPad which had his home page up. He was relaxed and satisfied. It had been emotional but seeing his parents when all was so good in their world was worth the trip. He was ready for the next one.

"Congratulations Robert on a successful visit into history. We trust it went well for you and that you can now trust us for another visit into history. Your interest in visiting Lincoln at Gettysburg on the evening of November 18, 1863 as he puts the finishing touches on his address is a worthy visit and if you choose to accept we will arrange for the visit next Sunday night, April 19, 2015, at eight o'clock," came through the ear buds. "Please acknowledge now."

"I accept," Robert said with no hesitation.

"Very good. Secure your gadgets and we will be start promptly at eight next Sunday. This visit will be for the full thirty minutes. Plan on one and one half hours. Donald is on your front porch. Good evening."

Chapter 17

Robert looked around the room but didn't move. The iPad showed 8:24 PM. All this had happened in twelve minutes. It had happened. He had seen and talked to his parents just as it was those years ago on his first day at MIT. They were as they were at that time. He had forgotten how pretty his mother had been and how handsome was his father. What a treat to see them that way, happy and full of life. The tears then came uncontrollably.

He recovered slightly, removed the ear buds and placed the small gadgets in their box and then in the zip lock bag. He placed them in a small section of the foam sound proofing that would hide them securely. Picking up his iPad he walked back into the main room and then onto the porch. Donald was there and Browser jumped up to greet him with a tail wagging exhibition that could only be interpreted as a maximum show of affection.

Donald looked relieved and gave Robert a gentle hug. "How did it go? Where did you go? Who did you see?" were his rapid fire questions.

"Donald, you won't believe what just happened. It happened. It really happened." Robert wasn't quite ready to explain it. He was still emotionally caught up in the moment. "I have to regroup a bit so let's just sit and talk about something else. It is for real. I can't believe it."

The sun had set and the evening shadows were turning to darkness. There were only a couple of street lights on but it was a pleasant evening and just sitting there was good enough, Browser had laid his big head in Robert's lap and was getting a good rub. Robert's nerves were getting settled and in few more minutes he was ready to talk.

He then told Donald the story from start to finish. Every detail. The tears came again as he described seeing his parents as they were at that time but he was not embarrassed by them. He explained to Donald about his mother's cancer and his father's death. For whatever reason this seemed to lift a burden from him and being able to tell someone in this way made him value Donald's friendship even more.

"I am going to visit Abraham Lincoln next Sunday evening at eight. I have some homework to do but I know what I am planning to talk about. I now have no fear about their technique but I have no idea of how they do it. The hypnotism is so fast and the transfer both there and back is almost instantaneous. I was under their control for less than twelve minutes and was with my parents for ten of that. This visit will be at the thirty minute limit, whatever that actually means. What a ride."

Donald just said, "Jesus, Robert!"

The two friends and the dog sat in the gathering darkness in silence for a while longer and then it was time to talk of other things. Everyday things.

"Jerry and Julie will be back tomorrow. The ship docks in the morning early so I assume they will drive home in the afternoon," Donald offered.

"It has been a fast eleven days, or I guess it was twelve total. How long have you known them?"

Donald paused and then said, "You know, I don't really know. Diane and I moved here when I first started my career in art. We met in college in 1978, got married in 1982 and our first six years I was in the Army. Luckily at a desk job in Fort Ord in Monterrey. I actually started painting while there. Lots of time visiting the galleries in Carmel. We bought our place here in 1988 and have been here ever since. Diane grew up here and wanted to come back. Jerry and Julie were here then and he first worked at the station and then bought it a year or two later. So I guess it has been twenty-seven years, give or take."

"They are nice people. Pretty trusting to let a stranger manage their business but I think necessity some time trumps common sense."

"Don't sell yourself short, Robert."

Chapter 18

Jerry walked into the station at noon the next day. He looked ten years younger than when Robert had last seen him. They exchanged greetings and pleasantries and then Jerry said, "You saved my life, my marriage, and my future. Boy, do I owe you!"

They both had a good laugh at the proclamation and then Robert replied, "You know what, I might say something similar to you. I really needed these two weeks and I would like to stay a little longer. Think we can work something out?"

"Let me call Julie," and without pausing, "She says you betcha baby. I will be down at five-thirty to check out and after we close Julie will join us for a bite at the Bakery and we will talk things over."

"You're on!"

Robert and Jerry closed up the station together, Julie was there at seven-thirty and the three of them crossed the street to the Bakery together arm in arm. The cruise had worked on Julie as it had on Jerry. Younger and prettier than Robert had remembered and he was greeted with a very nice hug and kiss on the cheek. He had been adopted as a sibling. It felt good.

Monday was a slow day, if you could call it that, at

the Bakery and all on hand came by to talk cruising. Robert's future plans would be discussed on the morrow but it was established that he could stay in the little house just two blocks away as long he wanted to, within reason of course.

As he walked home that evening he realized he hadn't thought about Sandra but briefly for several days. Checking on the iPad found Conrad's boat at sea rounding the point entering the Straights of Juan de Fuca. It would be dark and it was still at least eight to ten hours to Anacortes. The worry came back as did the over whelming desire to see her again. It was good he had some things happening in his life that could make his missing her less dominant in his thoughts. Those things were not permanent and if, and when, they lessened he knew they would be back.

The next morning he had his usual breakfast at the Bakery and met up with Jerry at the opening time at the station. He apologized for being side tracked at the Bakery last night but as things were slow first thing in the morning they could have a coffee and talk a bit. Jerry again thanked Robert several times and told him how much they had needed the break and what a good time they had.

Robert made the direct approach to get the conversation to what he needed. "Jerry, I need about si weeks more here in Point Reyes Station and I would like to stay in your little house. I don't have much cash and could work at the station for the rent. Would that work out for you?"

A big smile broke out Jerry's face and he responded "You bet your life. How about ten hours a week for the rent and fifteen dollars an hour for extra time? We can work out a flexible schedule almost anyway you want."

"Jerry, that's more than a fair deal. I appreciate it," Robert saying this as they shook hands.

"Julie did the books last night and told me we should book another cruise as soon as possible as you had the station the most profitable it has been in months. Couldn't be more happy. I know you will be moving on, or up, at some time in the future but you will always be welcome here."

Robert left it up to Jerry to do the scheduling but asked for Sunday afternoon and evenings free. It would work out fine.

That afternoon Robert stopped by Donald's house and told him of his deal with Jerry and that he would be in the house for probably the next two months. That was good news to Donald and he asked Robert to stop over that evening to talk a bit more. He thought he had something he might be interested in doing.

Robert then went to the used furniture store on the outskirts of town. Sitting right where it needed to be was a small bookcase. Just the right size to hold two medium sized boxes of books. An hour later the case was filled with his father's collection. They were nice books, mostly history, and many biographies of the men and women who had made a difference. They looked nice and the first two he selected were about Abraham Lincoln and written in the early 1930's.

His preparation for next Sunday was underway.

Chapter 19

The small table and one of the small chairs were getting a lot of use, none of which was for dining. Robert made a second trip to the used furniture store and found a larger table and a good condition office chair which fit his body just right. The table was a good size for a dining room table and he could now leave the small table in the sound proof room. He could roll in the office chair when it was needed there. The small sofa was more like a love seat but with a big pillow and his legs resting on the opposite arm rest made a comfortable place to lay back and read or take a quick nap. His little house was becoming a home. It would work for him.

The thought of Sandra here with him made him smile but he then thought that it might be not be right for her. The AIS showed Conrad's boat in Anacortes's Cap Sante Marina. They had made a safe passage and the rest of the trip would now be in the planning stage. He was hoping Sandra may have had enough sailing by now and would decide to stay on terra firma.

Robert walked over to the Bakery feeling very much alone. Just two weeks had passed and so much had happened. Suddenly his life had some routine, a future and now he felt alone again, but the minute he entered the

Bakery the loneliness disappeared.

After the pot roast special at the community table and a good walk about he landed on Donald's porch. The greeting by Browser was rousing and the hand shake with Donald was as it should be. They passed some pleasantries and Donald took Robert back into his back studio. He had a large sculpture in clay started which featured a life size swan in a pose that was very much like in the painting he had been working on the first time Robert had visited his studio. "Recognize it?"

"Sure do. It is looking pretty good. I didn't know you were into sculpturing."

"Well maybe I shouldn't be. It, the sculpting, doesn't really suit my temperament. Maybe it's just the medium but it is not coming easy. I can get the proportions right but the detailing just doesn't seem to click. I was thinking you might like to give it a try?"

"Me? I have never touched clay or a sculpting tool. Why would you think of such a thing?" was Robert's quick reply.

Donald smiled at this expected response. "You underestimate yourself. I have a knack for sizing up people and you have more talents than you know. Take this home with you and play around with the clay and the tools. Just experiment for a while and then finish the head for me." he said as he handed Robert a small box of clay and tools and then lifted the head off the big sculpture placing it on a soft foam pad in separate box. "Remember the longer you hold the clay in your hand the softer it gets."

Robert stood there without saying anything now holding what could be his future but not realizing it. "You're kidding me? Aren't you?" was the best he could come up with.

Donald went over to one of his bookshelves and pulled out "Sculpturing Birds in Clay" and handed it to him. "Everything you need to know. Come back in a week and show me what you have done. Don't let Abe take up all your time. You may surprise yourself."

When Robert got home he set his new project on the table and rearranged his Lincoln books and notebook on one side and spread out his new things on the other side. There was space on the table but his time would have to be divided. It was the time he wasn't too sure about but he picked up one of the smaller lumps of clay and started to squeeze it in his left hand as he walked around the room. It soon softened and he could pinch it easily into various shapes. It was soft, warm and malleable in an almost sensual way. He didn't realize it yet but another door had just been opened and he would be walking through it in a few weeks.

Robert brought up Sandra's email address on his iPad and started to compose a short letter to her. He wanted her to know he was alright and where he was. It should have been a simple matter. They had been so close and open with each other for that year but her choice to leave him left a doubt so severe that he was unsure of how to proceed. A number of back spaces had him back to 'Dear Sandra,' for the third time. He decided to try once more and to be direct. "I am 42 miles from our old apartment in SF in a small house in Point Reyes Station. It is now been two weeks today and so many things have happened my only wish is that you could have shared them with me. I will always hope that I will be at least able to tell you about them. Please let me know you are OK and what your plans are. I will be here for at least two more months and maybe much longer. This may be my place. Robert."

He read it once more and then touched the send button. "For better or worse, it was sent," he thought.

The lonely feeling came back. Despite all that was going on right at this moment he was sure he would trade it all just to hold her once more. To feel her body against him, smell her scent, hear her voice and see her smile. Just once more.

Chapter 20

He set the clay aside and tried to work out in his mind how to approach Abraham Lincoln on his next trip back into history. He had no doubt it would happen in the same manor that his extraordinary visit with his parents on his first day at MIT had occurred. This time he would have to be prepared. He had browsed through the two books from his father's library collection and found a number of interesting lines to follow but now he needed some more focus on how to proceed.

Lincoln's early life had been covered in detail and was of some interest but Robert was more interested in the mature man. He was tall, six foot two inches, although some times was reported as being taller than that. In any case he was very tall for the time having long legs, long arms, big feet, big hands and was exceptionally strong. He was not a graceful man and didn't sit a horse well, and for that matter even in a chair. It was said by many that it looked like his feet would drag on the ground unless the horse he was astride was a really big one. In a chair he always looked a bit awkward. He also didn't have much interest in his dress and was more comfortable in plain and rough clothing than the finer attire of the elite he became a part of. One could also state he was somewhat lacking in social graces. Add to all this was that he was not a hand-some man, homely was more descriptive.

But his eyes were his power. They had a soft gray look that could earn the trust of any man. He was a literate man with a good memory and well read but had little formal education. He liked to use words and liked to use short stories to answer questions. Apparently many of the stories were considered "rowdy" and not always suitable with some of the company he kept. Many were what the "Plow Boys" loved. It was said he could take their own stories and tell them back to them in a different way and they then loved them even more. He was one of them but they never suspected his genius. His voice was a bit high and often described as reedy but he could mesmerize his audience in any environment. Some thought he had two personalities, one at home with the common man and the other at the level of the elite. Occasionally he would mix up the two and find himself in embarrassing and humbling situations.

Robert was curious at what to expect of the atmosphere of the David Wills's guest bedroom. It was located on the second floor corner of the house with the stairs rising to the landing just outside the entry door. In mid November it should be cool, even cold, and heating would be by coal or wood. The dinner party that night would have been on the first floor with the attendant odors rising into the upper floors. Then there would be the human flavors of heavy wool and cotton clothing of which many may have been worn for a number of days. The smells might be the new experience as the visuals had some original records and the later photographic representations of the room had been seen many times.

Also to be explored was the health of Lincoln at the time. It was recorded he was ill when he arrived in Gettysburg and was sick for several weeks afterward. Robert thought his real discovery would be in how Lincoln made the final edits of his address and determining which copy he would use to read the address from. He wanted above all to convince Lincoln that his address would be treated as the great work it was and that his thinking that it would fall short for the occasion was not correct. Robert was not sure if this would violate the agreement of changing history but he didn't think it would.

He spent the next hour working on memorizing the address a second time, as he had done before in high school, in it's accepted form. His plan was to recite parts of this to Lincoln as he was making corrections to his text. It would be a fun exchange if he initiated a few of the changes Lincoln would have been making on his own. He was getting excited about his next adventure. He was actually happy. It was a feeling he hadn't felt in some time. "There is some hope for my future," he thought.

Almost unconsciously Robert picked up the clay and started squeezing it as he looked about his space. It was almost therapeutic. He picked up Donald's book on "Sculpturing Birds in Clay" and began thumbing through the pages. He had the clay and several of the tools shown. He read the initial instructions thinking them mostly common sense and was comfortable with what was being described. Picking up one of the small steel tools, the one with a pointed end of a long triangle and flat side opposite a rounded one. The other end of the tool had a long small diameter, oblong rounded point. It felt good in his finger tips and he made a few marks in the clay. He turned another page in the book and there was a gorgeous swan head sculpted in clay in the upper corner. Robert new immediately what was happening and a genuine smile formed on his face. He was in the right place, this was the right time, and he thought he had the right stuff. He had the chance for a new life and he was going to take it.

Chapter 21

The next morning the sun was shinning and there was none of the usual morning overcast. The orange juice had an especially good flavor, the sticky bun the best he could remember, and the coffee was just right at the Bakery. The conversation was good at the community table and he was at the station just as Jerry arrived. Even Jerry seemed happy and allowed he was a happy husband as everything was very good in his life this morning. They set up a schedule to have Robert open the station each morning at seven and Jerry would take over three hours later at ten. They would set special times as needed to allow each time off as required and Robert would always have Sunday afternoons off unless another arrangement was made before hand. A handshake sealed the deal and since Jerry was there Robert decided to take a long walk.

He headed out northward on Mesa Road and walked a mile or so and then decided to retrace his steps back to town. Down one of the straight away stretches he spied a familiar big man being pulled along by a big reddish brown dog. The man bent down, unleashed the dog and Robert prepared himself as best he could. Almost prepared, but once he was on the ground Browser let him know that he was his best friend ever. Donald walked up, had a good laugh, and got Browser back under control. "Robert, I have never seen a dog, any dog, act this way. Especially a well trained bird dog like Browser. What is it you have that no one else does? Not that I want any of it, but what is it?"

"Let me catch my breath," was the best Robert could muster as he sat up straight and was giving his best friend a good ear pull and back scratch. Getting to his feet he and Donald shook hands and started the walk back into town. The big dog just meandered along between the two men as if all was just right in his world as it was in theirs.

Robert filled Donald in on his schedule with Jerry and how that was working out good for him. Then a little more on his preparation for his visiting history to talk with Abraham Lincoln. Donald added his wish to go with him, as a witness but not as a participant.

Robert then changed the subject again. "You know something Donald, just handling that clay is a really good experience. I really like how it feels. How it softens when held in the hand. How you can shape it, smooth it out, work it into shapes. I browsed through the first part of the book you lent me. Looks like you gave me the right tools to start with and I am going to set the head up and start working on it. Hopefully I won't screw it up so bad that you will have to start completely over."

A big grin formed on Donald's face and he said, "I knew it. You don't know it yet but you are hooked. This is going to be fun to watch. You have some time right now to do a few things you have never had the time or place to do and I believe you may have the right stuff to do them."

Robert took in a big breath of Point Reyes air and slowly exhaled. "You couldn't have said it better, Donald.

In fact it is scary how right you are."

The two big men and the big dog wandered back into town then Robert peeled off to his house and Donald and Browser headed on to theirs, each feeling good about their lives.

Robert picked up his iPad and brought up the home page and the Mail icon had a nice little "1" next to the envelope so he touched it. The New Mail was a reply on the one he had sent Sandra yesterday. He was almost afraid to open it. He touched the open box.

"Dear Robert, I too have had two weeks I wish I could have shared with you. What I did to you haunts me and I don't want to admit to how selfish it was. Conrad has become a real friend, and I emphasize a friend. A change in plans will have us sailing to Alaska and then returning south towards San Francisco in August. Live your life as you want but maybe save a spot in August for me. It would be best to wait until then to correspond further. Sandra."

Robert read it a second time, then a third. Four months to wait, to not know exactly what she meant by a spot of time in August. Something was happening that had changed the around the world cruise to a much safer and shorter cruise up the inside passage to Alaska. He could think of several possibilities but would just have to wait to find out. The request to not correspond was difficult to accept but he could understand that somewhat. He would wait. All his thinking he could let her go and not see her again was gone. His calendar was now centered on a spot in August. August!

Chapter 22

Another perfect morning had dawned and as ten o'clock arrived so did Jerry. The schedule would work out just fine. Jerry liked his mornings to start slowly and by that time he was ready to meet the day. He actually liked running the station and all those he took care of liked both him and the services he provided. Robert was a morning person and his routine at the Bakery and opening up the station was a good fit. The rest of his day was then his own and he suddenly had found himself with much to do.

There was one problem looming. He was running out of money. On his arrival in Point Reyes he had no debts, about $2500 in his Chase checking account, $500 in cash and his Chase credit card paid up and still with it's $25,000 credit line intact. Chase didn't know about his current income situation. He actually had no outstanding debts or bills to pay until his next auto insurance payment was due, and that was over five months away. Other than his expenditures at the Bakery and the few things had bought for the house he really wasn't spending much. But until a few weeks ago he had gotten used to spending five thousand dollars a month and thinking nothing of it. Three thousand dollars looked mighty small to him now and he was sure something would come up to crash his world. No medical insurance sat in the back of his mind but so what was his thinking.

It was time for a trip to the local Thrift Shop as he needed a few things to supply his new sculpture venture. It was all of five blocks from his house so he walked. On entering he almost tripped over what he was looking for even if he wasn't really sure what that was supposed to be. A small diameter pedestal like table of a little over four feet in height sat just inside the entrance. It was an industrial type, a gray metal pipe with a twenty-four inch round plywood top that could rotate. Sitting atop this was a heavy cast iron disc that supported a arm with an extension that had a clamp to hold whatever it had been designed to hold. One look and Robert looked around to find the shop owner.

"How much are those things over by the door?" Robert asked of a small, weathered little woman who was sorting through a box of new donations in the back of the store.

"Oh! Those two things over there?" she pointed at what he was looking and pointing to.

"Yes!" was Robert's quick response.

"What are they? Came in yesterday and were left out back. My helper brought them in this morning and we were trying to figure out what they were. They are heavy. You want them?" she offered without much enthusiasm.

"Yes, I think I do," Robert responded.

"How about twenty dollars for both?"

"You got a deal," and Robert gave her a twenty. "I will have to get my van and will be back in a few minutes. I am staying in Jerry Gallager's house just a few blocks from here."

"Oh hey, you're Robert, the guy that saved Jerry's life, marriage and future. I should have given you a discount. All the girls at the Bakery talk about you all the time. Better watch out for a couple of them. I'm Mary, just Mary."

Robert let out a good natured laugh and shook Mary, just Mary's hand. Ten minutes later his sculpture stand was in place and the heavy swing arm had clamped in place a quarter inch wooden dowel supporting a clay swan's head. Perfect. So perfect a sense of unease found its way back into his mind.

After about an hour of detailing around the eyes, following some suggestions from the reference book, Robert thought he had made some progress. Not done yet but an improvement. A little more work near the eyes had them starting to look almost real. He was close to having it right and it was time to leave the work alone for a while. He began to sense that maybe he could do this. It was a good feeling to do something that had an immediate reward. It was direct with nothing between him and the finished product. At least with the original part of the creative portion of a sculpture.

He had a late dinner at the Bakery and had some good conversation at the community table. He met a man about his age who had stopped in on his drive to San Francisco from Washington state. He had just delivered a sailboat there and in a rental car was returning home to the Bay Area. He had the time and liked the drive down the coast on Highway 1 much better than Highway 101. It turned out he had delivered the boat to Anacortes and spent two days there getting it cleaned up and ready for the owner. His extra hand made the trip in reverse with him as he was returning to the area from down here. Worked out fine and they had been a good team going outside and under both sail and power had made good time.

Robert asked him if he had seen a Tartan 4700 named *Du-eT* in the Cap Sante Marina and he said he had. It had left early yesterday and he didn't have a chance to meet the owners. Beautiful boat, one he could only dream about. It wasn't on his dock so didn't get to take a close look.

"It had a couple on board but I couldn't tell about their relationship. They didn't seem like a married couple or a father and daughter combination. Something didn't look quite normal but I can't really tell you why. Just a feeling, you know. The lady was very attractive but looked tired and the man somewhat disheveled. She was at the helm. Seemed an odd couple for cruising but there are all types on the water."

Robert wanted to know more but didn't want to press the issue. "I worked for the guy in San Francisco for about a year. Didn't realize he was a sailor. Actually he never mentioned any interest in sailing so I was surprised to hear about him buying a boat and heading out to sea. It was rumored he wanted sail around the world."

"Well I can guarantee you that those two will never make it around the world. The boat is capable but my impression is their sailing days are numbered. Understand that's a gut reaction. You can never be sure but something there doesn't seem to me to be quite right."

He stood up to leave and Robert asked "Do you have a card? I may need some help with a boat in a few months, maybe in August, and it would be handy to have someone who knows what he is doing to help out or give some advice. I'm Robert Johnson."

"Sure. Alan Parsons," giving Robert his card and shaking hands. "Nice talking to you Robert. Hope our paths cross again."

Robert sat still for a few minutes mulling things over. He now had another worry to add to the list. He did have a card, Captain Alan Parsons, with telephone number and License Number. No address, just San Francisco.

"Hey Robert, you okay, good looking. We are closing soon," was a cheerful voice in his ear and a very nice smile from where it came.

"I'm good Suz. Thanks for taking care of me," and he stood up and headed to the little house just two blocks away.

Chapter 23

It was Saturday. Tomorrow was Sunday, April 19 and Robert had a date at eight o'clock. He needed to do a lot more preparation to be ready for his visit with Abraham Lincoln. He had plotted out his strategy but needed to study up on what he was planning. It was simple in theory but more complicated in fact. Almost since Lincoln gave his "few appropriate remarks as Chief Executive of the nation to formally set apart the cemetery grounds to their sacred use" what exactly were his spoken words that became one of the best known speeches in American history.

There were five manuscripts of credit, all written in Lincoln's own hand, but none of which matched exactly. And none that matched witnessed written recollections. They were the Nicolay, Hay, Everett, Bancroft, and Bliss drafts each named by the recipients last name. Only the first two, Nicolay and Hay, were written before the words were spoken on the afternoon of November 19, 1863 at Gettysburg. This was Robert's primary focus. Could he determine which was read by Lincoln that afternoon. The internet and "Wikipedia" were his references. He had polished his memorization of the address but it was the Bliss draft as it is the accepted copy for use. It was hand written and signed by Lincoln but months after the actual event.

Robert realized before noon that trying to compare the Nicolay and Hay manuscripts on his iPad was difficult to do and he needed a print copy of each. A fifteen minute visit with Mary, just Mary at the Thrift Shop solved that with a nice Epson printer, which came with a bag of ink cartridges, and was on his table printing in less than an hour. Two hours later he was still confused. He had until eight o'clock tomorrow night.

He needed a break so a walk about was in order. The sun was getting low in the West and the coastal colors were starting to do their thing. Robert let his eyes relax and let the colors wash over him. What a good feeling it was. How fortunate was one to have a few moments like this. He found a bench along the trail side and sat down. His eyes started lose focus and a few tears formed. He wanted Sandra to be here. He was hoping beyond hope that he was right about this. He wouldn't let himself think otherwise.

Robert was in position. The iPad showed 7:52 PM with Sunday, April 19, 2015 just below. The small box with the devices sat nearby. He was relaxed but his anticipation level was high. He had come to a layman's conclusion that the Nicolay draft would be the reading manuscript for the address although the general consensus was that it was the Hay draft, or possibly another that Lincoln had written the night before, or the morning of, and had then been lost. There was no doubt that the Bliss draft had been chosen early on as the official manuscript. It was what adorns the Lincoln Memorial, the one Robert had memorized in high school, and was even referenced in both the 1930 books on Lincoln in his father's collection.

He was going to find out in the next few minutes.

7:55 PM, then 7:56 PM blinked on. Robert still felt relaxed. He wondered how he could be. What a unique position to be in crossed his mind. One week ago this minute he thought the whole idea of tripping back in time was ridiculous and he was waiting for some kind of sales promotion or a super "gotcha" banner would be displayed on the iPad. Now he sat calm and patient. 7:59 PM and then 8:00 PM.

"Hello Robert. Welcome to your next visit into history. Are you ready?"

"Hello John. Yes I am."

"Robert, we are probably more excited than you are about this visit. We have been following some of your research and think this will be the best visit using this program so far. We can't tell you how good it has been working with you. Fix your ear pieces and set the transmitter/receiver piece next to your iPad. Let us know when you are ready."

Robert inserted the ear pieces, positioned the transmitter/receiver and said in a firm voice, "I am ready."

The expected pattern filled the iPad screen, started revolving and a muffled voice spoke a word or two he couldn't discern. He next found himself in a room with a bed with dark head and foot boards. A big man dressed in some kind of night shirt was sitting on it with his back to him.

Chapter 24

It took Robert a few moments to adjust and he then said, "Mr. Lincoln I am Robert Johnson."

From the man on the bed came, "Well hello Robert Johnson, good to meet you. Come over here and let's size each other up."

Robert had just an instant to get his bearings in the room. He was just inside the closed door to the stair landing. The bed was centered with it's headboard against the wall to the left and the fireplace was opposite that wall. To the right of the headboard was side table with a basin, water pitcher and a hand towel on a bar. Two windows were in the wall directly facing him. A small round writing table and chair to his left. A chest of drawers against the wall to his immediate left and on the other side of the bed was a large Queen Ann chair. Just past the fireplace was a second access door. A third door in the corner to his left may have been to a closet. All in all a very nice room.

"Yes Sir," said Robert and he made his way around the foot of the bed. Lincoln had stood exhaling several grunts and met him shoulder to shoulder at the corner. Robert felt no contact but Lincoln acted as if had made solid contact. "Okay Robert, call me Abe. We are the same height. That's good. I like that. I am not feeling well so I will just sit back on the bed and we can talk a bit. That all right with you?"

"Sure. That is why I am here. I thought you would be working on your address for tomorrow."

"That? That's pretty much done. Fact is, I think it is ready. Not much of a speech but then as I was asked to say just a few words after the Honorable Edward Everett orates for two hours, or more, so that may be too many anyway. Want to hear it?"

Robert almost fell over, or thought he might. "Yes Sir, I would certainly like that."

"It's Abe, Abe!" Lincoln picked up two pieces of paper off the bed next to him, placing one on top of the other. The top showed "Executive Mansion" stationery, the heading clear to Robert. A thrill ran down his spine. The second he couldn't see clearly but it was a different paper. They were conventional letter size paper of the time about five and a half by eight inches. The writing was neat and in ink on the top page and there was one correction in pencil on the last word or two in the last line. Robert recognized the Nicolay draft.

Abraham Lincoln, in his night shirt sitting on his bed, cleared his throat with a just perceptible cough and began, "Four score and seven years ago . . . . " he read on until he got to, "It is rather for us, the living, we here be dedicated," he stopped mid sentence and told Robert he had made a small change to this line. "I wrote this part yesterday in Washington. Anyway I had to finish it up here an hour ago. Forgot to put in some extra sheets of stationery so I used some regular paper. Had to even get that from Nicolay tonight, and a pencil too, to finish up with. Can't remember anything anymore. I'm not that old yet!

Guess I am getting there."

After moving a bit to get more comfortable Lincoln continued. "Anyway the whole address was in my head so all I had to do was write it down. Let's see, where was I?" Lincoln shuffled the two pages and got the second, lined and penciled sheet on top.

Robert almost fainted when Lincoln read the last words " . . . . . that we here highly resolve these dead shall not have died in vain; that the nation, shall have a new birth of freedom, and that government of the people by the people for the people, shall not perish from the earth."

The two of them held their positions, Lincoln on the bed and Robert standing just a few feet away. "Well, what do you think?" Lincoln asked Robert.

"Tomorrow, read it exactly as you have it written. Don't change anything. Not a single word. Not a word!"

"Well, you are rather positive of that. It seems to me to be a bit on the short side and not, what's the word I want, grand. I think I need to do better but I don't feel too good and I am dead tired. I will look at it again in the morning."

"Abraham Lincoln, don't change anything. Don't let anyone talk you into changing one word. Trust me on this. History wants, needs, and must have these exact words!" Robert was almost shouting and Lincoln looked shocked.

There was a minute pause as the two men looked at each other. One surprised at what was said to him and the other surprised that he would say such a thing.

Lincoln spoke first. "Robert, I will take your advice." He folded his two page manuscript in three folds, rose and walked over to his coat placing it in the inside pocket. "No changes," he said with a nod and wry smile to Robert.

It seemed the room quieted and Robert could see that Lincoln was tired and needed sleep. It had apparently been a nice Indian Summer day in Gettysburg and the two window sashes were open. The Street noises in the town square out side were getting louder as 10,000 people had arrived already and three times that were expected by the morrow. Robert went over to close the windows and re-membered he could do no such thing. Lincoln seemed not surprised by this and struggled off the bed and closed them then headed back and climbed into the bed lying at an angle with his big feet hanging out uncovered. He was a big man thought Robert.

"I have a question for you Abe. Do you have one more answer left?"

"Probably, if it is short one."

"My great, great grandfather attended one of your Lincoln-Douglas debates. It was either the Ottawa or the Freeport. He was fifteen years old at the time and lived in Troy Grove. His dad gave him a dollar and told him to go learn something."

Robert could see a smile form on Lincoln's face and decided he wasn't such a homely man.

"He described how Douglas was a short man neat-ly attired and after his presentation he couldn't see how you could answer." Robert then decided not to include how Lincoln had been described by the fifteen year old as sitting in his chair with his big hands hanging between his bony knees and his head sunk between his shoulders like a sick turkey buzzard during Douglas's opening remarks. "He described that you then got up, and after a hesitant start, answered all his points and showed where they were wrong. Before you had finished the crowd went wild and would have followed you anywhere."

Lincoln's smile got bigger and he sat up and said "That was at Ottawa, the first one. It wasn't a good debate and that little smart ass hit me with a bunch of questions in his rebuttal that I didn't answer exactly but I got him back at Freeport. I sure got him back there." He laughed out loud and laid back down.

Robert heard the first ping and knew he was short of time. "Abe, you won't remember me being here tomorrow. Could you place your coat on the big chair open with the manuscript sticking out of the pocket in plain sight. When you wonder why your coat is there instead of hanging up and see the manuscript it might trigger the thought that it is the one to read from. Could you do that for me."

Lincoln groaned and rubbed his eyes. "You are a hard taskmaster my man but that's a good idea." He struggled out of bed and laid out his coat, opened it up and pulled the manuscript half way out of the pocket. Turning to Robert he said "That about right?"

Three pings hit Robert's ears. "That is just right."

Lincoln climbed back on to the bed and tried to get the blanket straightened out and over himself. His head was on the pillow and his body awkwardly angled across the bed. Robert walked over and looked down on him. His eyes were closed and his breathing was heavy and sleep had come.

Robert's last thought was that Abraham Lincoln was a beautiful man. His next thought was his iPad showed 8:34 PM.

Chapter 25

Robert sat frozen in his chair. He was reliving his meeting with Abraham Lincoln. It had gone by so fast. Not how he had planned but it couldn't have been better. He was having an emotional let down when the voice known as John came through the ear buds.

"Robert, that was a fantastic meeting. We are overwhelmed at our end. Thrilled. It was great. Great. How are you doing?"

"I am okay I think. It was so real. Everything. And Lincoln was magnificent. I can't think straight right now." Roberts's voice was cracking and he was starting to shake. He was crying and was afraid he was having a breakdown. "John, I need some time here. Give me a few minutes."

"Robert, how about you take a day and we will contact you tomorrow night at eight as usual over your iPad. We can compare notes then. It was extraordinary and we are delighted. Will that be okay for you.?"

"That will work for me. I'll get myself together. I am alright, I think."

"Donald and Browser are on the porch. We will talk tomorrow evening."

Robert took another five minutes then put away the devices and closed his iPad down. He stood up and felt just a hint of imbalance and steadied himself holding the back of his chair. A few more deep breaths and he regained his composure and went out on the porch. Browser was at the door looking up at him with his big tail sweeping in a fast rhythm.

"Well Robert, how did it go with Lincoln?" was the needed voice of Donald sitting in the chair next to the one waiting for him which he slumped into holding onto it's arms with a tight grip.

"You won't believe me when I tell you about it. Give me a few more minutes. Donald, you won't believe it."

They sat in silence. Browser positioned himself so his big head filled Robert's lap. It was dark and almost no sounds disturbed the night. Robert's world started to return. The shaking was over and he began sensing the need to talk. Donald was there, right where he was needed.

But Robert couldn't get the first sentence formed. Each start never got to his lips. Donald picked up the task by asking "Have you ever visited Gettysburg?"

"One time on a high school field trip. That was the civics class that had us memorize the Address. I didn't really appreciate the geography or the monuments."

Donald let out a sigh and offered "In 1984, I think it was summer time, I had a work trip to Washington. Don't even remember what it was about but the military sent us on some silly assignments. They were sort of like paid vacations. I rented a car and on a late Saturday afternoon I drove over to Gettysburg. Maybe a two hour drive. Along the highway when I got there was a sign to some battlefield so I pulled off and parked. There was a stone fence with a style and I climbed up the three steps and down the other side and walked out into the middle of the field. It was just starting to get dark and a mist like haze came in and everything around me took on that gauzy look like in a fog. It got very quiet and I had this weird feeling come over me. I sat down and waited. Nothing happened but I could feel this almost overwhelming sense of doom. Like the thought of death covering me like a blanket. It was scary. In the fields around Gettysburg some seven to eight thousand young men were killed and four or five times that many wounded in three days of fighting. Was it their ghosts? I can remember that feeling right now. It still scares me. I went back to my car and drove back to DC and I have never been back to Gettysburg, nor do I ever want to go there."

Robert thought this over. His visit was concentrated on one subject, Lincoln. He had been successful but as he thought about it he realized he had no sense of anything but Lincoln's presence and their conversation. He saw the room, the furnishings, Lincoln's clothes, his body, beard and his eyes. But no recollection of any odors or sounds other than their voices. No sense of temperature. No sense of fear or anxiety. Just his exchanges with Lincoln. Maybe that was how it was meant to be.

Robert then looked at Donald and started his story. Minute by minute, second by second, every detail from his first consciousness of being in the room until he was back in front of his iPad.

"That's quite a story, Buddy. That is some story. You should write it down just like you just told it to me and keep it as a record in a safe place."

They sat there for another half hour and then Donald gave Browser a gentle kick with his toe and they headed home. Robert stayed seated for another hour and then went inside. His iPad showed *Du-eT* was at the dock at Rosario Resort on Orcas Island in the San Juan's, Washington State. Robert climbed into bed, closed his eyes and saw Abraham Lincoln asleep.

Chapter 26

Monday went by as it should. Robert spent some time working on the Swan's head, experimenting with various techniques on feathering. After a few hours it was getting close to what he wanted but was still not there yet. He closed up his sculpture studio, more accurately identified as half of his dining room table and his new sculpture stand, and decided he needed a break.

His visit with Lincoln had taken a lot more out of him than he had anticipated. He was really tired for the first time since he had been in Point Reyes. It wasn't the physical work but the mental stress and not sleeping well last night. His mind seemed not to able to relax. He was used to being able to compartmentalize things but this time his thoughts kept running over each other. He was hoping after tonight's visit with his mentor things would get straightened out.

His morning at the station had gone well. He had not told Jerry about his trips back in history and planned to keep that to himself and Donald. Donald had agreed to be his silent and only partner for now. He picked up some groceries at the food market and found he already knew most of the people there via his regular visits to the Bakery. Point Reyes Station was a very small town. He liked it.

This day's lunch was on his porch and was a peanut butter and jam sandwich, made on fresh Bakery bread, an excellent apple, potato chips and a diet Coke. That helped and after he had leaned back in his comfortable chair he took a fifteen minute nap. He then drove up the west side of Tomales Bay on Sir Francis Drake Blvd as far a Seahaven. As he passed by the Resort & Marina he mused that there might be a slip there that could berth a forty-seven foot Tartan. It was a nice day and towards it's end he had started to relax.

At 8:00 PM he was in front of his iPad in his proper place. "Hello Robert," didn't even surprise him.

"Hello John, I am feeling much better today than last night. It took most of the day but I feel much better about things now."

"That is good to hear. We have a plan that I think you will like. But first, that was an extraordinary visit with Lincoln. You probably don't understand how excited we are working with you. You have a gift with people and under the conditions we are working it makes us confident that your visits will all turn out excellent."

"Thanks for that and back to you and your team."

"Robert, here is what we have come up with for your records. We record your visits in real time. From the time you enter the place until you return. We transcribe the recording in real time at four seconds per line and adjust the font size from twelve New Roman to fit each line. This means that a thirty minute visit will end up with about twelve pages of single spaced script. From this a normal dialog can be generated and presented in a variety styles. We will provide you with a copy of the script and it will be yours to use as you wish. It will not be copyrighted."

"John, that is something I could really use. I wasn't sure I could write it up without making mistakes and omissions and that it wouldn't be a good record. That will be great."

"You probably also understand it would be best not making it public until we get a little further down the road on the project." John paused and then added, "Robert, we estimate that our 'travelers' will be limited to at most five trips with three or four probably a safer number. We are monitoring your vitals on each visit you make and if we detect any problems we will take the appropriate actions."

"I won't ask how you do this or what is implied. I will trust you and your team. I assume the ear devices are very special."

"As we have said, you are the best traveler we have worked with yet. Have you another visit in mind. We have a date picked out a week from this Sunday, May 3, at eight o'clock. Will that work for you?"

"Yes. That will be fine. I am working up a visit with Leonardo da Vinci on April 29, 1519 in his room at Clos Luce in Amboise, France. I am thinking in the late afternoon. I plan to discuss many of his accomplishments that withstood the test of time and several of those that came about. This will be just days before his passing and historical records cite he was still mentally alert at the time. I want him to know how much of his thinking was four hundred years ahead of his time, that many of his inventions came into being and that his notebooks are still in use, studied and admired. Also, if time permits, I want to tell him how my father fell in love with Mona Lisa when he was alone with her in the Louvre Museum as a boy."

"Robert, that sounds like a very good project and you are officially on the schedule. The Lincoln visit transcript should be in you Inbox now. Good evening."

"Good evening, John."

Robert checked his Email and there was one item shown to be in the Inbox. He touched the box and a PDF download icon showed. Touching resulted in a first page of script with no title or date. Just a series of conversational sentences, punctuated and spaced by time increments. There were spaces and lines that were blank or just with one word or two words. He swept through all twelve pages and the pattern stayed the same. It was what was said by both Lincoln and himself and he thought by filling in his remembrances and thoughts he could produce an accurate and complete story of his visit. Taking some liberties with possible thoughts that Lincoln might have had he could develop a very entertaining and informative record.

He was delighted with the prospect and printed out two copies and moved the download to Archive. "I have another project to work on and have become a very busy person here in Point Reyes Station. I wonder how all this will turn out. I need a partner in this. Sandra, I need you here," were his thoughts.

Chapter 27

Robert had and needed a few days of almost lazy activity. His morning hours at the station were just enough to get the morning underway. He spent some more time on the sculpture of the swan's head and by mid-week thought it ready to show Donald. He hadn't started writing up his "Lincoln Visit" and had decided he needed a better computer and word processor program to compose it on. A trip to the Thrift Shop did not disappoint and there now sat on his table a good condition Dell laptop loaded with Microsoft 8 and Word. It had a wireless connection to the internet and he soon had set up access. At one hundred and fifty dollars he thought he had made a good bargain and nothing had showed up that didn't look like what should be expected. His first entry on Word was A VISIT WITH ABRAHAM LINCOLN and that was all for the moment.

He walked the half block to Donald's place and knocked on the door. There was no sound from inside or any indication that Browser was there. Robert thought he needed to get a phone. Not an iPhone, for Christ's sake, a telephone. That will be next and then I will have to think in terms of a mailing address. "But maybe I should wait until after May third." he muttered under his breath.

As he left Donald's porch he could see the familiar shape of a big man with a big dog. He prepared himself as the shape of Browser came into focus at full speed. They met in a good connection this time as Browser was learning that a slide and stopping just short the collision point got to the rough petting and ear pulling faster. Donald walked up and greetings were exchanged.

"I think I have the head about right. Have you got time to take a look at it."

Donald smiled at that and answered, "Bring it over and we will stick on the neck and see how it fits."

"Great! I'll be right back. I have a little more to tell you about my Lincoln visit and what is in the planning," Robert said as he headed back to get the head. Browser started after him, then stopped and looked back at Donald. Donald hadn't moved and after one more look towards Robert's departing figure the big dog returned to his master. The two of them stayed where they were and in a few minutes Robert was back holding a swan's head on the ¼ inch dowel and Browser's tail was again flailing the air at high speed.

Robert very carefully handed the dowel to Donald. Again he mused that the big man's large fingers could so gently take the it from him. He held up the head and rotated it for a thorough inspection.

"You did it. I knew you had the touch. Knew it. Let's go put it on the bird and see where we can go with this."

Donald sounded genuinely pleased and they headed to the studio space in the rear of the house. He picked up a pair of pliers, clamped the dowel and then slid it in position on the neck of the swan. A soft push had the head in place and angled correctly for the pose. The entire sculpture came to life.

"Yes!" was all Donald said.

Even Robert was taken back at what a difference what he had done with the head did for the overall sculpture. His eye went directly to the eyes on the swan and the difference was so great that he let out a gasp.

"I didn't think it would make that big a difference. Does that always happen?"

"Not always, and if it doesn't you have to start over again," was Donald's immediate response. And then, "How would you like to finish the bird for me? I will do the environmental parts, the water, cattails and grass. I would like you to do all the detailing of the feathers."

"Sure. I think there is something in this for me. Something I desperately need in my life right now. I appreciate you leading me there." Robert said this with confidence.

"Let's go take a seat on my porch this time and discuss the meaning of life, or if that's too much trouble you can tell all about Lincoln."

They assumed their positions on the porch. Donald brought out two cups of coffee and Browser had a noisy session at his water dish and then laid his wet mug in Robert's lap. They each were in the right place, and it was the right time, to sit back and relax. And that is what they did.

They sat, sipped some coffee and looked across the street at the several houses and porches without focus. Browser got his head rubbed and seemed to doze off and Robert felt as good as he could ever remember. Finally Donald said "Bring me up to date my adventurous friend."

Chapter 28

Robert told Donald of the transcription document he had received from the project and what he was thinking of doing with it. He agreed with the idea of embellishing the accurate text into a story format and suggested a book if the other adventures worked out. The idea of a visit with Leonardo da Vinci really excited Donald and he wanted to participate in the planning if this would be okay. Robert indicated he would build an outline and they could go over it together. Thirty minutes wasn't much time and a number of different approaches would be good as talking with Leonardo could lead in a variety of directions. Donald liked that idea and would have plenty of time in the next week and a half as he had someone to handle the hard part of his current sculpture that was falling behind schedule.

They fell into a more personal conversation as Donald explained Diane's absence the last few weeks. "Diane is a good artist in her own right and is doing pretty good selling her work but her true talent is in selling, and teaching others how to sell. In fact she is so good at teaching her main income is now from holding seminars. Her start was, of course, selling my work. We were both busy starving artists when we moved here but I was developing faster than she was and had a more unique style. I can't sell anything. She spent most of her time working on promoting mine and as you can see it worked out. A lot of artists have the same problem and she is doing seminars on how to sell your art work almost every week scattered about the Bay Area. Too many this last two months but she has cut back her schedule and will be around home more where we both want her to be."

Robert offered that they had a good partnership and that he still had hopes that Sandra might be what he needed in his life.

Donald surprised Robert in saying he had been following *Du-eT* on AIS. Robert told him of his meeting Captain Parsons in the Bakery and his opinion on seeing the boat and Sandra and Conrad at Cap Sante Marina.

"You know, Robert, I think something is going on there more than a sailing adventure. I've done the round the world and the Inside Passage trip they have now started. Let me tell you something about both. I think most men, if they have spent any time around the big oceans, have a gene in their brain that says 'go to sea, young man.' Most never do, they just dream about it. Or can't afford to do it. Conrad had the chance to do it and could afford to do it. But you need to have someone else with you unless you are truly a masochist. Sandra just happened to be there. Something has happened and I think Conrad has a time limitation. I would guess it's a health issue."

"I haven't told you I emailed Sandra. I asked if she was okay and if she needed anything that I was here. She answered she was good and they were heading to Alaska and would be returning to San Francisco around August. She wrote to live my life as I wanted but could I save a spot for her in August."

"That I would do, my friend, that I would do," was Robert's gentle giant's response.

They sat for another hour watching the shadows lengthen and the colors change. A large V of Canadian geese flew over head high in the sky. Donald commented they were a few weeks early but that it was quite a sight.

Then "How about we get our big bird over to your place?"

"Let's do it. How are we going to do that?"

"You just watch."

Back in the studio Donald positioned the big sculpture a bit and fiddled underneath the plywood Formica topped board on the sculpture stand. Then he placed a small pry bar with a block as a fulcrum and up popped the swan away from the water and foliage.

The two of them lifted the swan on it's board away from the stand and set it on a table. He then pointed out another sculpture stand that was table high and they carried it over to Robert's place. Leaving the door propped open a round trip had the Swan in position for Robert to work his magic. It took only fifteen minutes. Robert thought things seem so simple when you know what you are doing.

Chapter 29

Robert's morning schedule was becoming a routine of breakfast at the Bakery with the other regulars at the community table, opening the station and working there until Jerry showed up which was almost always by ten. The rest of the day was at the house dividing his time between the sculpting projects, Donald's and starting two of his own, and working on the travel back in time project. Other than the station schedule he was on own his time and could pretty much do as he pleased.

He worked up the manuscript of his Abraham Lincoln visit in an organized fashion. In Word, he copied the entire script he was provided which included all the spoken words and punctuation. He then wrote in all he could remember of the details in the appropriate spaces and coordinated them in a descriptive story style. He then edited to make it all work. After about three readings, and making changes and adjustments, he decided to view it as finished.

He printed out two copies of the double spaced forty-two page manuscript, one for himself and one for Donald. He also made a PDF copy and emailed it to himself and then placed it in iBooks on his iPad. Sunday afternoon he was invited to Donald's for dinner and he presented him with his copy of *A VISIT WITH ABRAHAM LIN-COLN* in a stationery binder.

Diane had fixed another superb feast, this time of some of last years venison. Robert hadn't realized how good well taken care of and prepared wild game meat could taste. He had a chance to get better acquainted with Diane and decided that the Connors were people you wanted as friends. They were a generation older than he but you wouldn't have thought so by the relationship that was forming. His travel back in time was not brought up but his manuscript was talked of as an attempt at fictional writing and he asked Diane if she would read it and give him an opinion as he was already starting a similar one on visiting Leonardo da Vinci. She was delighted to participate and quickly selected a book from her library on da Vinci that she thought he might find helpful.

Later in the evening Robert talked to them both on the progress he was making on the Swan. He had been experimenting with lining the feathers and made a couple of tools from two metal hair combs he found at the Thrift Shop. Using a very small file he was able to sharpen the teeth, and then cutting the combs to various widths, make very nice lines in the clay that looked realistic. He was making good progress and wanted Donald to take a look in the next day or two. Even Browser thought the evening had been about as perfect as it could be and behaved as any finely trained bird dog should.

That night he clicked on the AIS icon and found *Du-eT* was at a dock at the Vancouver Rowing Club in Vancouver, BC. Google Earth showed that location just opposite the famous Stanley Park and within walking distance of downtown Vancouver. The thought of Sandra having such an adventure with another man was the first time he had ever felt envy. It wasn't jealousy, it was envy. He would trust her as to the physical relationship with Conrad but that he was enjoying this adventure with her instead of him was what hurt so much. "I guess envy and jealousy are similar. I can handle the envy but I won't let it become jealousy. I couldn't handle that," was Robert's thinking. On the AIS the boat icon just sat there at the dock but knowing who was on board hurt. He closed the page and just stared at his home page, lost in thought, for half an hour.

The next morning after his station duties Robert realized he was falling behind in preparing for his meeting with Leonardo. He was having some doubts about how to make his approach and remembered how Lincoln was able to change everything when he asked if he would like to hear him read his address. He needed to take into account for an event like that if it occurred. He picked up the book Diane had loaned him and spent most of the day reading. Everything pointed in the same direction. He was going to meet and talk to one of the greatest minds in human history. A nervous shiver ran down his spine.

Donald came by in the late afternoon and took a quick look at Roberts progress. "Dammit, I can't believe you could have the skill to do work that good. Ticks me off because it takes most people years to get there," he grumbled out but he was smiling.

"I take it you like what you see?"

"Yes, yes and yes. It is looking so good you will have to sign for the work, too. I can't claim anything that looks like that just for myself. I've seen this once before. A young kid from a cattle ranching family in Wyoming, or maybe it was Montana, came to a sculpture class I attended. It was a one week beginners class and we each were to do a small sculpture to finish as a graduation goal. His was so good that everyone stood around and just thought there was no reason to try to compete. The instructor took it over to the local foundry and before the first casting was completed it was sold. One of the better galleries got wind of this new talent and signed him up. For most of us entering into the arts profession it takes years to develop the skills and even longer to gain entry into the gallery world. He started at the top and has never looked back. Don't you do that to me!"

Robert could only smile at this. He had just done some feather detailing, not real sculpturing.

Chapter 30

He now had less than a week and Robert had decided on a approach to take in his visit with Leonardo da Vinci. The fact of his genius was not in dispute. The breadth of his talent and abilities was beyond comparison. Some might consider it was his curiosity that lead him into so many fields of endeavor, which was obvious, but it was his genius that resulted in what came of the study and understanding of that which interested him that set him apart from all others. Robert thought that just wondering how can that be done was not the same as doing it, or why is that to discovering why it is. The fact that Leonardo started so many projects that often were not completed, and were often revisited a number of times before finished or discarded, seemed perfectly normal to Robert. A mind such as Leonard's would be so active that no matter what he was concentrating on at any given moment it would have been constantly interrupted by other, or many other, thoughts to be investigated.

He would have only thirty minutes with Leonardo which seemed an almost infinitesimally short period to talk, especially with how near he was to his death. Robert decided he would start his approach by introducing himself as a person from five hundred years in the future. He would hope that Leonardo would accept this unbelievable claim to be Heaven sent and not resist it's suggestion. He would quickly move to tell Leonardo that his painting of *Mona Lisa* is the most recognized painting in the world and in the Christian world *The Last Super* is the most revered and renowned. He would then tell him of how the bound copies of his notebooks and writings are equally famous, still in use and printed in dozens of different languages. And of the numerous museums that display his works in all their forms and the fact that the bed he now lays on is part of museum that features many of his inventions in constructed models.

This was to help Leonardo have an answer to a lament he made often in his notebooks. "Tell me if anything was ever done. Tell me if ever I did a thing. Tell me if anything was ever made." Robert was hoping at this point he could help him answer this questioning. He was sure Leonardo already knew the answer to the overall question as his earned place in society of the great artists and thinkers of his time should have already allayed these fears. If it was his scientific studies and inventions he was referring to it would make more sense. It was here Robert planned to talk of airplanes and submarines and hoped to describe the concept of the internal combustion engine that was the missing element that he needed to power many of his ideas into reality. That wouldn't happen until some 300 years later. He was that far ahead of his time.

"Only thirty minutes. I will have to say all this just right or this visit may fail," was Robert's thinking. He decided he would ask Donald to help him. It could work and the only purpose was to ease Leonardo's departure. "Maybe this is just selfishness on my part but it may lead into a good conversation," Robert muttered this aloud and was glad there was no response.

On Thursday afternoon Donald stopped by to check on the Swan and was without Browser. He had a dentist appointment and the big dog was left at home sulking. Robert missed him but he needed some quiet time with Donald so he would have to make it up to Browser on his next visit. The review of the Swan went well. It was done and Donald couldn't hide his enthusiasm. "That is really good. You have a touch, Robert. You even made a couple of adjustments to the neck and the left side near the tail. It works. The feathering is perfect."

"You got me hooked. I've started two small works which I will show you next week. I need some more clay so can I borrow another pound or two?"

"Sure, let's go get it now and we can get set up to get the bird back into the pond," Donald said eager to get his sculpture back together again and finish it up.

"Do you have a few minutes to talk Leonardo da Vinci first?" Robert asked.

"Of course. My mouth is still numb from Novocaine so I don't really want to do much for a while any way."

They sat in their now usual chairs on the porch. Robert filled him in on what he was planning and Donald agreed it would probably be a good approach. Then he brought up one of da Vinci's more famous unfinished works, *Saint Jerome in the Wilderness.* He described to Robert the fact that it was used in art school lectures both as an example of da Vinci's procrastination tendencies and his interest in anatomy. He is always quoted about the necessity of the artist knowing the underlying anatomy if he expects to accurately position and represent the body. Next is always how he kept hauling the unfinished board about and making changes, such as with the tendons in the neck years later. Donald suggested it may have been more what many artist find that what they have originally envisioned for the painting just wasn't working but that it was good enough to maybe fix later. He would drag it out when he had some down time, mess around with it and then come to the same conclusion again and store it back somewhere in his studio to work on again later.

Donald suggested "I wouldn't bring that one up or anything on the subject of not completing works. This is a sore spot to any artist. Some things just don't work out right and no matter what you try it just doesn't work. It is true in art and it is true in life."

"I think one should remember that little bit of wisdom," Robert agreed.

The two of them sat on the porch in silence for a few minutes then Donald continued. "Robert, da Vinci not completing *Saint Jerome in the Wilderness* brings up another aspect in the visual arts and that's demonstrated by Michelangelo's *David*. It is ranked right next to the *Mona Lisa* and *The Last Super* as one of the greatest works of all time. But *David*'s head is proportionally too large for his body and his right hand is large in itself and larger than the left hand. Those facts, however, in no way detract from it's magnificence. When you view *David* in person there is no question that it earns it's place as one of the greatest sculptures in the world. It is almost over powering. It is over powering. But one can think that if Michelangelo had been working in clay he might have lopped off that right hand, sat down in his studio and sculpted another to match the size of the left. One could also imagine he might look at his finished *David* and think 'I made that damn head too big.' What da Vinci would do is probably stash it in the back of his studio. But with a seventeen foot marble sculpture, at over six tons, and two years of work one would have to be satisfied with how it came out. And how it came out is without question as it should have."

For the moment nothing more needed to be said. The two friends sat very still, each with their own thoughts about Robert's next visit into history.

Donald then stood, gave Robert a crooked smile, and excused himself. "You have added a new dimension to my life that I cannot, and will not, share with anyone else. Thank you." and he stepped off the porch and headed home.

Chapter 31

Sunday morning, May third, arrived on schedule as one would expect and Robert felt he was almost ready. The two previous days had been a whirlwind of activity. The Swan sculpture had been completed. Placing the bird into it's environment went without a hitch until it was decided by both of them that it's position should be angled about ten degrees more forward. About two more hours were required to make the new placement and the judgment had been correct.

Donald wanted Robert to share in the signing but he thought it would be best to have Donald's name alone. It was his client that had made the commission. Donald told him about selling the Swan painting to one of his collectors, even before it was finished, a few weeks before Robert had seen it on his first visit. The request by the collector for a bronze in the same pose had been discussed at that time and he had accepted the commission to do it.

"One always over estimates one's abilities when a nice commission is offered," Donald offered. The buyer was expected in an hour to pick up the painting and approve the sculpture. "I just got the painting back from my print people yesterday. It will done in edition of a hundred fifty and that will be very profitable for me. It is counter intuitive but that makes the value of the original much more, so everyone is happy."

"I think I am learning a lot here. I assume a print doesn't cost nearly as much as a bronze casting and selling one hundred and fifty prints is a lot easier than selling fifteen castings. Am I missing something?"

"Don't you tell anyone about that. In fact it would best if you put that thought out of your own mind for now." Donald was smiling but it was good advice.

He put his signature in the clay with a flourish and marked the date and next to a blank space a back slash followed by fifteen on a prepared area on the back side of the sculpture. The door bell rang. Browser barely lifted his head. Donald looked at Robert and said, "It is not you, my friend."

Introductions were made and the collector loved his new and beautifully framed Donald Connor original watercolor. It was then to the back studio and the enthusiasm continued. Donald gave some credit for Roberts's help which was barely recognized by the collector as he was as in love with the sculpture as he was with the painting. Robert excused himself and left Donald to work with his customer. He knew he had just witnessed something very few get to experience and wondered if he could ever get to that point if he pursued a career in sculpture. "I will have to give this some very careful thought," Robert was thinking as he let himself out the door that hid Donald's empire.

Entering his own empire, it seemed pretty small. It was now early afternoon and he was hungry. Peanut butter and jam felt right, was prepared and quickly consumed. He sat down in front of his iPad in the sound proof room and touched the AIS icon. *Du-eT* appeared in the Jervis In-let heading in bound. Robert searched Jervis Inlet and photos and a map came up. It's most highlighted information was that it lead to the Princess Louisa Inlet through the Malibu Rapids. There was information on the history of it's naming and discovery, but it was the photos and YouTube offerings that occupied Robert for the next hour. The beauty of the place and seeing it in a video from a boat level sent him into an emotion of envy again. He shut down the iPad and decided he needed a short walk.

Robert hadn't gone fifty steps when he heard the familiar "woof-woof" coming from behind him. Turning in time to grab a big head and squeeze a pair of extra large and floppy ears gave him what he really needed at that moment. Browser did his magic and Robert's day got suddenly better.

Donald told him how well it had gone with his collector. He had loved the sculpture and ordered the Number one of the planned fifteen castings. Donald then handed Robert an envelope, which contained a nice check, and his day got even brighter. They retreated to his porch and took their respective chairs and after a very long time at the water dish, Browser assumed his spot and soaked Robert's pants in that most inappropriate place. The conversation was mostly about tonight's visit with Leonardo. Robert outlined a few more thoughts which were mulled over. When Donald headed home he told Robert he would be outside at eight-thirty and Browser gave him a most sorrowful look.

Robert was set up in front of his iPad at 7:45 PM wishing he was some where else. Maybe on a sailboat docked just a few hundred yards from "Chatter Box Falls" in Princess Louisa Inlet, British Columbia, Canada. "Could it be that all of this was leading there," floated through his mind. 7:51 PM blinked on the screen. He better get ready. He thought he was and he reviewed his opening gambit. If it worked the rest should go alright. 7:58 PM, 7:59 PM, and then 8:00 PM.

Chapter 32

"Hello Robert. Welcome to your next visit into history. Are you ready?"

"Hello John. Yes I am."

"That is good to hear. Your visit with Leonardo da Vinci is set up. He is in ill health, as you know, and you are correct in that he is mentally alert. It should be a fine visit. He was one of the greatest minds in human history. We trust you are looking forward to the visit as are we."

"I am inserting the ear pieces now. The receiver-transmitter is in position."

"Have a good visit."

The screen went to the concentric circles and lines and Robert's last view was 8:05 PM. He found himself in a very open and sparsely furnished but plush late fifteenth century bedroom dominated by a big canopied bed draped in red velvet on each of the four dark wood posts. Directly in front of him was a writing table with a single chair fronting it on the opposite side from where he stood. An enormous fireplace was to the right and assorted seating chairs and stools were along the walls. The floors were a beautiful arrangement of colorful red to orange bricks within rectangular borders of multiple blue colored bricks. He thought for a moment he was in a painting by Vermeer.

In the bed was Leonardo da Vinci, asleep.

Robert was uncertain what to do. What caught his eye was an open doorway to his right which lead to the dining room and on the far wall was a familiar painting that he was sure was da Vinci's *Saint John the Baptist*. He took a few steps closer to get a better look and on the middle of the wall, between two windows, was the *Mona Lisa*. Whether it was his gasp in recognition, or his foot steps, a voice from the bed asked "And who might you be?"

Robert spun around and positioned himself next the writing desk and said, with a slight quavering in his voice, "I am Robert Johnson and I am visiting you from five hundred years in the future."

"Is that so Robert Johnson. Come over here closer so my tired eyes can see you better. Five hundred years in the future is quite some period to span. I bet you know something I don't. Let's talk about it."

Robert gulped down a big breath. This was going to work and he quickly went around the desk and came up to da Vinci on his left side. His head was on a big pillow and was raised at what looked like a comfortable angle. His large white beard was in waves and looked as if it had been combed out minutes ago. His face was clean and his skin looked quite good for a man who was supposed to be near death. Best of all were the eyes. Maybe a slight cloudiness but bright and showing a welcoming curiosity.

"Pull up one of those stools and sit down where I can get a good look at you. Now what are you doing here?"

Robert approached, but remained standing, and started without hesitation. "You understand I am from the future. Two Thousand Fifteen to be exact. And today, just as it has been for a hundred years, your *Mona Lisa* is the most recognized and valuable painting in the world."

Leonardo da Vinci tried to laugh. It was a slight choking sound, but it was a laugh. "Is that true? Really true Robert?"

"Yes, it is true."

"Did you look in the dining room over there," a wrinkled and slender index finger pointing towards the doorway Robert was looking through when da Vinci first spoke.

"Yes I did and she is more beautiful than ever. Is that *Saint John the Baptist* on the next wall?" Robert asked.

"Yes! I like you Robert Johnson from 500 years in the future. What else can you tell me."

"*The Last Super* is almost as famous as the *Mona Lisa*," answered Robert.

"How can that be? A few years ago the paint was falling off the wall. I tried a different technique on painting on plaster and it worked for a few years until the the paint started to fall off and showed me what a bad decision I had made. Pretty damn embarrassing. It's something I don't even want to think about."

Robert smiled at this and knew this was going good. "A whole series of restorations went on over the years. The painting was so good and loved that every time it was thought to be lost some one, or some group, would have a try at restoration. The last really big attempt was less than 50 years ago. This was an all out effort to save it and 20 years was spent working every possible modern technique. This time they have done it right and the painting is beautiful beyond belief. You would think it was as it was the day you made the last brush stroke. It should last for centuries."

Leonardo blinked several times and Robert saw a tear come down his cheek. "They loved it that much," was all he said and remained silent for a few moments.

Then as with a burst of new energy "What of my inventions, my writings, my notebooks. Is any of that left, or is it just my few paintings?"

"Leonardo, listen carefully. Your writings, sketches and drawings have been preserved and copies are bound in books and notebooks. They are read and discussed world wide, in almost all languages. You are as famous for them as for your paintings. And your inventions. Let's talk about them," Robert got this out in an excited voice.

Leonardo's smile shown through the beard and his eyes sparkled. "Which ones? Which ones worked? Did anything actually lead to something?"

"You know you accomplished a number of things during your life that were of your design and invention but let's talk about flying. Men flying." Leonardo's look made Robert know he had hit the right subject.

"Did it happen? It couldn't be the way I was try-ing. A man can never be a bird. He is too heavy and not strong enough to overcome that. But I wanted to fly, Robert, I wanted to be able to fly."

Chapter 33

Robert knew this was what he had hoped to talk to Leonardo about. He started "You came so close but you didn't have the right materials to accomplish the task. They didn't come into being for another two hundred years or more. Your glider idea was on the right track. It was not flying, but it was developed about fifty years ago, my time, with new materials that allows men and women to leap off high places and with the right air currents glide for long periods, sometime hours when all is just right. It was air against gravity but it worked. You would have loved it. It is more a combination of your parachute idea and the glider. Just as the big birds soar with out moving their wings it is a single wing with the body stretched horizontally below it."

Leonardo closed his eyes and whispered, "I can see it. I could have done that with silk and a thin wood frame like a kite. No trying to flap the wings, just sail on the up drafts." His eyes then opened wide and he continued, "How about true flying. Did that happen?"

"Yes it did. It is now called an airplane. There are all sizes. Some for just one man and really big ones for hundreds of people." Robert's pause was interrupted.

"How did they do it Robert? Describe it to me."

"Leonardo, it required something that didn't get invented until about the year 1800, almost three hundred years from now. It is called the internal combustion engine. They are now in my time so common, and taken for granted, that no one thinks about them at all. They power all sizes of cars and trucks, like your carriages and wagons. A small one may be equivalent to the power of one hundred horses. It would take less space than your writing desk and weigh less than a man."

"How can that be? That's impossible. How does it work?" Leonardo sounded exasperated.

Quickly Robert started with "Imagine a cup with no handle with a shaft connected inside to a cross dowel. The other end of the shaft to a pedal like on your bicycle design. Now push the inverted cup up into a tight fitting pipe. Close the upper end of the pipe but leave a way to pump steam under pressure into the space above the cup."

"Yes, Yes! It would push the cup down and cause the pedal to crank. I can see it. There is more to it but I understand what you are saying." The excitement was back. Robert was truly impressed. It wasn't a very good description but Leonardo had grasped it immediately.

"There is a lot more but what really made it work was a fuel derived from oil that could be mixed with air and ignited to do the function of the steam."

"Internal combustion engine. I like that, internal combustion. Tell me more."

"Just imagine placing four of the pipes and cups together and altering the combustion cycles so they could push the pedal in a way to provide a rotary motion to a driving shaft."

"Yes! If that shaft was the axle of a carriage it

would rotate the wheels and the carriage would move. I should get some paper and draw some sketches."

"Leonardo I don't have much time left with you and I want to tell you about the airplane before I go." Robert knew his time was running out but he hadn't heard the first ping yet. Robert could only imagine Leonardo's thought process as all the new science was coming into focus for him.

"Tell me Robert. Before you go describe the airplane. I don't have much time left either but to know that man can actually fly would be a fine thing for me to know."

Robert knew he had to hurry this and started hoping it would be adequate. "First imagine a thin walled tube big enough to hold two chairs side by side inside such that you and I can sit next to each other. The tube should be about twenty feet long tapered towards the rear to a rounded point. Extending from and connecting to each side of the tube, about opposite our chairs, are long bird like non flexible wings. In the front end of the tube is a small internal combustion engine whose driving shaft extends forward. Attached to that shaft are two opposed paddles, a propeller, with their blades angled to pull the plane forward when rotating at a high speed. At the tail end of the tube is a small wing extending on either side and a single vertical wing on top. The whole plane is supported on the ground with two wheels under our chairs and a single wheel under the tail. What do you think?"

"Let me start at the paddles. Just like paddles in the water. With the right angle and moving them fast enough and they will pull the airplane through the air. If the wings are right in area and angle they will then lift the plane off the ground when the plane moves forward fast enough. Moving the tail wings in angles up or down will move the plane up or down relative to the horizontal and moving the tail vertical wing will turn the plane left or right." Leonardo was beaming with his understanding. "Robert, what a gift you have given me. I don't understand a lot of this but I now know it can be done. If I was at the right time I could have designed such a airplane. It could be built and I could fly it. That is all I need to know about man flying." Leonardo laid his head back and closed his eyes. Robert heard the first ping.

"Leonardo, there is one last thought for you on flying. There have been a few men who have built very light airplanes that by using something like your bicycle design and propellers have flown under their own power for short distances. It is not practical but it is a beautiful sight. It can be done."

"Thank you Robert. That was most enjoyable. Thinking again like I used to be able to do, but I tire and will close my eyes for a while."

Robert heard the three pings. He looked down at Leonardo da Vinci now asleep again. What a nice and interesting man. A beautiful human being. The next moment he was staring at his iPad screen. The screen showed 8:35 PM.

Chapter 34

Robert, just like after his return from his Lincoln visit, sat very still facing his iPad but not really seeing it. His thoughts were just starting to form in that his visit with Leonardo da Vinci had gone well and it may have been a success. He felt the emotional let down and assumed there was a rational reason for feeling this way when John voice came.

"Robert, you have done it again. Fantastic. You have such a good rapport with your subjects. That you can converse with the greats with such ease and have them interested and conversational is a true gift. We are delighted. How are you doing?"

"John, about the same as with Lincoln. For what ever reason I am feeling a let down, maybe even depression, but it seemed to go well. Even easy, although I didn't get the chance to talk submarines with him which I know he would have liked."

"You know he will have no memory of your visit or of any part of your discussions. But when da Vinci thanked you for giving him the chance to think again like he used to be able to do we all let out a cheer. What a gift that was. Congratulations." John was so enthusiastic it made Robert smile and immediately helped his mood.

"I needed to hear that John. That helps."

"Robert, shall we make contact tomorrow evening at eight to talked some more or would you like to continue now? Donald and Browser are on the porch."

"Let's go for tomorrow. I need some time right now. I am feeling a little queasy at the moment. Not sick really, just a little off."

"That will be fine. Tomorrow at eight."

Robert spent ten minutes just trying to relax and focus. Neither was coming easy. He put the ear buds and transmitter/receiver in their box and stood up to put them in their hiding space and lost his balance. Grabbing the arm of the chair, and trying to keep from falling, he staggered behind as it rolled over to the wall and stopped. He was breathing hard and knew something was not just right. He sat back down and let another ten minutes pass until his senses seemed to return to normal. He stood very slowly this time, making sure his balance had returned, and then walked slowly to the front door.

Browser was there looking up directly into his eyes, searching, then the big tail started it's wagging and Robert felt assured that he was back, or at least close to being back. Donald's welcomed voice asked the expected question "How did it go this time, my friend?"

They sat on the porch and Browser's head was on Robert's lap. Having the big dog's ears to pull and head to rub helped Robert get comfortable and then he started the conversation with Donald. "You know what surprised me the most was the space and the luxury of Leonardo's quarters. Beautiful rooms, not a lot of furniture but everything looked like it belonged. The *Mona Lisa* was on the dining room wall as well as *Saint John the Baptist*."

"You are telling me you saw them both, right there in front of you. Jesus Robert, what a thrill that must have been." Donald said almost choking on the words.

"I didn't have time to get close as that was when da Vinci woke and asked who I was. He has a great voice and didn't even act surprised when I introduced myself from five hundred years in the future. He just calmly asked me to come close so he could see me better and that five hundred years was quite some period to span."

Robert then went on detailing his visit with Donald quietly listening.

"What a story Robert. He understood your description of the engine and the airplane. Just like that. What a mind to be able to think that clearly on what had to be so foreign to what was general knowledge of the time. If he had a few more weeks he would have sketched it all out. He would have built himself a hang glider and jumped off a cliff to fly."

"Donald, part of the program is that the visited have no recall after the visit. There can be no opportunity to change history in any way. But you are right, I am certain he would have done it. At least building the hang glider. A successful flight with his beautiful beard flying is somewhat more doubtful but fun to contemplate."

They sat for a while longer and Browser slept peacefully. It was dark with a faint light from a street light. Then Donald asked Robert "How are you feeling? You look tired and something else is not just right. Are you okay?"

"Yeah, I think so. When I first stand up after about ten minutes of recovery time my balance still isn't very good. In fact I almost fell this time. It seems to get better quickly and I feel pretty good right know. You would be surprised how much it means to me to have Browser greet me at the door and talking to you helps immensely. I will be talking with John tomorrow night at eight and I will ask him about this. He has already told me five trips is maximum which only leaves me two more."

"Maybe you should be satisfied with three."

Browser roused himself with a big stretch and yawn, looked at Donald, then at Robert and then back at Donald indicating it was time for them to head home. And that is what they did.

Chapter 35

At eight the next night Robert was sitting in front of his iPad when John's voice spoke the "Hello Robert" that was expected.

"Hello John. I had a good day today and am looking forward to your comments," was Robert's response.

"Good! Leonardo da Vinci was as good, or better, than Lincoln. We are so satisfied with these two visits we cannot express it in words. Just great, Robert. The transcript should be in your Inbox. It should be no surprise to you that we have a copy of your Lincoln manuscript. You should become a writer, Robert, you have the talent."

"Wonders never cease to amaze, I think the saying goes. Thank you. I will be trying to do the same with the da Vinci manuscript this week."

"That will be great. Robert, understand, we do plan to compensate you at some point. We are operating a very experimental operation here and are not sure how to proceed with what we are accumulating from these visits. The value is there but we are not quite ready to try to monetize it. We hope you understand our position."

Robert thought this over and quickly responded, "I do understand and it really doesn't concern me at all. As for being a writer that is another direction I never thought

I would take but it is most enjoyable in the doing. It is a path I could take. By the way, are you into publishing?"

"That is a good one on us. But let's leave it as a maybe. Have you another visit in mind?"

"Right now the answer is no but I have several I am thinking about. I need a few weeks to put together a possible. Will that be okay?" was Robert's best answer as there was more on his mind on the effect these trips were having on him.

"Robert, we have been monitoring your vitals during your visits and find several elevated points on your return that are of concern. They are not permanent but are worrisome. The problem of balance is the symptom."

"John, are you able to read my mind?"

"Not really, but we do know what we are doing and we are trying to be very careful with our travelers. We spoke earlier of how many trips are safe. We think you can safely take one more trip without any damage but think two is the absolute limit." John's voice was very calm but serious.

"How sure are you about that?"

"We are sure one more trip for you will be safe. The balance problem is common and only temporary. During the thirty minutes travel your brain, and therefore your body, is essentially non-functional except for the autonomic nervous system. It is like being in a deep hypnotic sleep. When you first awake, or in this case return, it takes a few minutes to get the consciousness functioning again. Standing too quickly causes the problems in balance. It is very similar, and related, to problems in aging. Our concern is the relationship of conscious brain function and autonomic function in separation. Since the symptoms seem to get worse on each return we have the five visit limit. Our experiments have shown this to be the correct number. You seem to be having the normal reaction so far and following your vital signs we are confident you are safe for at least one more visit, hopefully two."

Robert took this all in and decided he would go forward. "Let me work out a next visit. Can we talk a week from tonight at the usual time? I should have the da Vinci manuscript done by then."

"That will be fine with us. Until next week."

The home screen appeared although Robert could not remember what had been on the screen just before then. A quick touch of the AIS icon showed *Du-eT* still at the dock in the Princess Louisa Inlet. He had read there was a three night limit at the docks and thought he would want to stay there even longer. August seemed to be years away.

The Inbox showed a message and the download icon came up, was pressed and there was the transcript. Robert browsed through it and the conversation was just as he remembered. It would be easy for him to write his next manuscript just as he had written up the Lincoln visit. What a delight it had been. What an extraordinary adventure. "I am one lucky guy," he said out loud.

Chapter 36

A VISIT WITH LEONARDO DA VINCI went quickly. It was almost a format with Robert being able to flesh out the conversations with his remembrances of the place and da Vinci himself. He enjoyed the challenge and in about twenty hours over four days had it pretty much finished. This time he decided to have Donald and Diane both edit it for him. A few corrections of spelling, grammar, punctuation, a re-phrasing or two, and it was deemed ready. The forty-six page manuscript was printed in two copies and they were bound in stationery folders, neatly titled. Robert added his copy next to Lincoln's in his bookcase with his father's books. He also again made a PDF copy and emailed to himself placing it in iBooks. He figured that John now had a copy but he would ask him anyway the next time they spoke.

As the enjoyment of writing and the reward in completion started working on his psyche he thought that writing might be something to pursue. Reading the manuscripts a second time left him satisfied with his efforts.

Thursday had somehow arrived while Robert was working on his manuscript and he hadn't touched his sculpture project. He had worked up two squirrels in action poses as two squirrels might be when chasing about.

They were just roughed in on wire armatures but he had the poses right and was ready to start bringing them to life. Then Leonardo came into his life and sculpturing had exited. The squirrels looked at him, although the eyes were not yet in place, and said, "hurry up we are bored in this position." Robert turned them around on his stand so they would be looking outside and took a break from his writing to check a few things on line.

The AIS showed *Du-eT* at dock in Lund. Sandra and Conrad had either made a long trip from Princess Louisa Inlet to Lund or more probably spent the night of the sixth at an on the way location. Google Earth showed Lund a neat place and they had a spot on the dock. The next big attraction would be Desolation Sound. The internet had lots of information on the many, and wonderful, sights to be found there. The little green image of envy popped up again. Robert clicked off the iPad and sat on his couch looking at two unfinished squirrel tails.

He was no nearer deciding on his next person of interst to visit than when he told John he hadn't picked one out yet. Sergei Rachmaninoff in music had come to mind as a major candidate, just as Claude Debussy would be. Thomas Jefferson, or George Washington, was on the list but they were too close to Lincoln. Jefferson would be interesting at Monticello towards the end of his life. Actually Mount Vernon was also an interesting place but Robert thought Jefferson would have more to offer. Christopher Columbus as he lands in the New World. Maybe even Vancouver as he explores the Pacific Northwest or Lewis and Clark in Oregon. Amelia Earhart on her last flight with Fred Noonan or Edmund Hillary and Tenzing Norgay on the top of Everest. The names and events kept popping up but none seemed quite right. He wanted an interesting individual who really made a difference in his or her contribution to history. Lincoln and da Vinci were such easy choices. They and their time and place were just right. Just what he was looking for again.

A walk with Donald and Browser was needed so one was arranged and taken. Robert posed his problem to them both and the three of them shuffled along one of the foot trails near town. It was a perfect afternoon as the sun shown and the Pacific offshore breeze was just enough to bring the smell of the ocean on shore but was not enough to dampen them or their spirits.

Robert then asked Donald "My great, great grand-father, Darius Johnson, the one that attended the Lincoln-Douglas debate in Ottawa, Illinois, was a true pioneer. He served, and survived, start to finish the Civil War. Met his fifteen year old wife to be while guiding a wagon train from Iowa to Kansas. They married a year later, had five children and he passed away a successful grain farmer on his farm near Marquette, Kansas. Would a first person's life story be of interest, or value, in today's world?"

"I would think so, but not in historical context. Maybe, but my bet right now would be Amelia Earhart. She had it all going for her and you might even find out what happened. Not sure about the timing. You wouldn't want to find out the exact place where she disappeared."

"The only problem with Amelia is time and place." Robert answered and then continued "I have to establish the time within reason but the place has to be accurate. Unless I choose them before they take off on the leg to Rowland Island I have no exact place and the only real reason to make the visit would to gain some insight on

where and why they went down. It would be a hard inter-
view when you know what is about to happen."

"Next!" was Donald's comment.

"I am leaning towards Rachmaninoff or Debussy.
Interesting times and characters, gifted musicians with lots
of history around them and their times. They left us with
their works which we still enjoy," Robert said, almost
sounding convinced.

Browser barked at something in the the bushes.

Donald agreed.

Chapter 37

Monday night, the eleventh of May, arrived before Robert was really ready. At exactly eight John's voice came over the iPad speaker. "Hello Robert."

"Hello John."

"Robert, we read *A VISIT WITH LEONARDO DA VINCI* and are delighted. It as good as the one of your Lincoln visit and you know how excited we were about it. Have you decided on your next visit?" John's voice was just a bit high and he was talking faster than Robert remembered so he knew he was sincere.

"Thanks for the review. I assumed you had access and it doesn't bother me that you do. As for the next visit I have almost decided on Sergei Rachmaninoff, with Claude Debussy a close second. What is your thoughts on those two?" Robert waited, but just for a few seconds.

"We tend to think Rachmaninoff would be the better. Do you have a time and place in mind yet?"

"No, I have to give it some more thought. Late in life would be best but part of my interest is his life just as he was making his plans to leave Russia and I want to spend some time studying that aspect. One of his down periods might also be interesting because to tell him of his later years success would be a nice part of the visit. I want to think on this some more."

"That is fine with us. How about a week from tonight with the visit planned for the following Sunday, May twenty-fourth, at eight o'clock?"

"That is a go. I will have the details for you Monday next." Robert was relieved to have some certainty and to have some time to get his life a bit more organized.

The goodbyes were said and were brief as usual.

He leaned back in his chair and thought about his thinking his life being more organized. His life was organized. It was not that it wasn't, it was that what he had to do was a group of small accomplishments that had no real future. Each morning a few hours opening Jerry's gas station. His initial efforts at sculpting in clay a pair of cute squirrels. The exciting adventure of visiting history which had at most two more trips before being finished. The possibility that he should try his hand at writing, but what genre or could he do it at all? And when, and more importantly if, would Sandra come back into his life?

He had found a place here in Point Reyes Station that he was comfortable with but other than the Connors and Browser he was essentially alone. Sandra was the key. He could stay right here and do what he was doing but if she did not come back into his life he would have to re-think what to do. Sitting in the sound proof room waiting for something to happen was not good enough. He thought of his father climbing Mt. Everest and thought he now understood why he had done it. He was humbled by this. A sadness overwhelmed him and he picked up his iPad and went out on the porch.

It seemed darker than usual and as the Home Page lit up it almost blinded him. He touched the Mail Icon and then New. Entering S gave him the only address he had there and he touched that and her address was entered. He typed three words, "How are you?" then added Robert and touched send.

Covering the iPad the darkness descended as did his spirits. A half hour went by and he thought he might as well head for bed, cover his head with the blankets and try to think of something positive for tomorrow. One last look on the screen and the little red circled "1" was on his In-box. He touched it and it was a reply. It was just five words, "You best plan on July." followed by "S". He now had something to think about under the blankets. He had no idea what, but it was closer in days and would make the time he remained in limbo that much shorter. A glim-mer of hope.

As Robert sat down at the community table the next morning, and his orange juice, sticky bun and coffee were set before him, he felt much better than he had the day before. The sun had come up and he had fallen asleep last night with some hope that whatever was happening with Sandra, he was still in her thoughts and hopefully in her plans. If it could be worked out he was willing to try. His life had been so good those months they were together that he had to find out if they could be that good again. Something was happening on the boat with her and Con-rad that he still didn't understand but he would find out in July. He could live with that.

After the morning at the station Robert decided to work on the squirrels. Progress was fast and the clay seemed to go on quickly and in the right places. By early afternoon they were looking pretty good. No details but much happier little fellows. He was thinking he could do this but that was enough for now. A long walk was in order and he covered about ten miles. It was time to put in time on Rachmaninoff and he had already decided his course. He had some granola and an apple for dinner and then started his on-line search. There was a lot to read.

Chapter 38

For the rest of the week Robert divided his time, spending his late mornings on sculpting and the afternoons and evenings on Rachmaninoff. He took breaks for long walks, several with best friends Donald and Browser, and the days started passing quickly. By the weekend the Squirrels were looking good. They would only require some final finishing and minor adjustments to the pose. Rachmaninoff was forming into a visit that might work. It had been a good 4 days for Robert and he was going to set his Squirrels aside for now and concentrate on preparing for his next visit into history.

Robert was using the internet to become familiar with Rachmaninoff as music had not been part of his formal education, nor had it been more than a casual interest of his parents. Preparing for Lincoln, a more familiar figure in history, he had at least some knowledge about him. Most Americans would know the name, who he was and have had heard of the Gettysburg Address. Leonardo da Vinci was a step up but you had to have been rather poorly educated to not know who he was. The name and work of Rachmaninoff would be very familiar to classical music lovers but for most it would be pretty much just the name. Robert fell into this class. He liked classical music but for the most part it was only in the background.

It took Robert only a few hours of research to realized that Rachmaninoff was someone he wanted to know. And just a few more to realize that this would as important to him as da Vinci had been. He didn't want in any way to fail to do justice to the visit. Each revelation brought him closer to a reverence of the man. What an extraordinary life he had lived and what an incredible musician he was.

Rachmaninoff was born on the first day of April, 1873 near Novgorod, Russia. There may be some question on the exact date but Robert thought it a nice coincidence that the month and day were the same as his. He died on March 28, 1943 in Beverly Hills, California just four days short of his seventieth birthday. It was what happened in and during this remarkable man's life that made him such an interesting person to visit some seventy-two years later. Robert would make his visit at his house at 610 Elm Drive, Beverly Hills, California during his last week, possibly Monday March twenty-second in the early evening. He was dying of an aggressive melanoma and in pain and discomfort. Hopefully the timing would work and that he would be able to provide a little bit of happiness for him in the thirty minutes they could talk. Robert would depend on John's research to set another date and time if this one wasn't thought to be right.

Sergei Vasilevich Rachmaninov was born into a noble family and was the fourth of six children. At the time the family had five estates, mostly from his mother's dowry, but by the time he reached ten years his father had managed to lose all but one due to a number of his personal and character short comings. His mother guided his early musical training starting at four years old. It was continued at the Saint Petersburg Conservatory and then completed at the Moscow Conservatory in 1892, with him winning the Great Gold Medal for his opera *Aleko*. He was praised and promoted by Tchaikovsky but when his first symphony was poorly received and the Russian Orthodox Church opposed his planned marriage he went through a period of depression for three years. He did marry his cousin Natalya Alexandrovna Satin on May 12, 1902 and they had two daughters, Tatiana and Irina. Natalya and Irina were at his side when he passed away.

It was from the time he came out of his depression that Robert's real admiration for Rachmaninoff came into focus. He composed his brilliant *Piano Concerto No. 2* and then started a life that can only be looked upon as phenomenal. He rapidly became one of the most famous of the Russian pianists and composers of the era and was in constant demand both in Russia and internationally. Of course, then came the Russian Revolution, World War I, the Great Depression, and World War II. Through it all he came out successful in the best sense of the word. Robert could only think that his own problems of the last couple of months were nothing. Nothing at all in comparison and he was embarrassed to even think he had problems.

Rachmaninoff was busy, in 1903 and 1904 he was the conductor at the Bolshoi Ballet and in 1909 made his first tour of the United States bringing with him his *Piano Concerto Number 3*. Success was his and his reputation was as one of the greatest pianist and composer of the time. Then the Russian Revolution of 1917 raised it's ugly head and with it the Soviet government. With an invitation to give a concert in Stockholm, Sweden, having his estate destroyed by the communists, on December 23, 1917 he left Russia with his family. With a few cases, filled mostly with books of sheet music, he left everything else behind never to return. In 1918 they emigrated to America.

Rachmaninoff then became a music and money making machine. He made over a hundred recordings and gave over one thousand concerts in America alone between 1918 and 1943. He became one of the highest paid concert stars of the time. He travel frequently to Paris, Dresden, and Lucerne. On the shore of Lake Lucerne he purchased property and had a villa built. New York City was home but in the early 1940's he spent some time in California to be among many of his Russian friends who had moved there. After renting a property for a short time he bought the Elm Drive home just over a year before his death. It was quoted that he was so enamored by this house that he said, "This is where I will die." It was to be a sad prophecy.

He was an extremely generous and kind man and had a dry sense of humor. In public, and when posing for photographs, he never smiled. One observer described him as "Six feet six inches of Russian gloom." He was tall but claimed to only being six foot two inches. Robert felt that most photos of him with others would make that the more likely. He did have big hands, with long fingers, which made it possible for him to reach chords that would be a problem for other pianists. As for the gloom, photos and movie film of him with family and friends showed him happy, engaged and a loving husband and father.

With this background information Robert thought he was ready to plan out how he would approach this visit and he was ready to commit to John on the date and place.

Chapter 39

Sunday, after opening and then turning over the station duties to Jerry, Robert decided to take the rest of the day off. He picked up a sandwich to go at the Bakery, stopped by the house for a few things, then got in the van and headed towards the Point Reyes National Seashore. He needed a long hike alone to clear his mind and just get lost in nature. Even though it was Sunday, and at first he had lots of company, a few miles of separation did wonders. At a small clearing with a view of a long stretch of the beach and the Pacific Ocean he found the spot he needed. The sandwich tasted good, the apple crisp and juicy, and the view was fantastic. Brilliant sunshine with a breeze that was just right. He was able to lay back and think how good it was to be alive.

That night at home he was still feeling the positive effects of his outing. He had found YouTube sites featuring Rachmaninoff's music. A dozen or more. Just a touch provided minutes of great piano, and piano and orchestra, renderings by various artists and venues. Several, by the master himself, playing his own works. Robert brought up the home page as the music played and tapped on the AIS Icon. *Du-eT* showed up as anchored in Laura Cove in Desolation Sound. He smiled and for the first time thought of

Sandra being there as a good thing and that maybe things would work out in a favorable way in the future. He needed that feeling and he thought maybe knowing Rachmaninoff was why he felt this way.

Monday night found him in position watching the clock tick down on his iPad. At 8:00 PM John's "Hello Robert." came as expected.

"Hello John." was Robert's answer.

"How is Rachmaninoff's visit coming? Have you a time and place?"

"John, it is going very well. The more I research the more I want this visit. Time and place would be early evening on March 22, 1943 in the north east upstairs bedroom at his house at 610 North Elm Drive, Beverly Hills, California. The bedroom is shown as bedroom number three on the public house layout drawing."

"Well Robert, that lines up very close to what we have in mind. We may want to study the time of day a little more but otherwise agree with what you have decided on. Following your search history has lead us on a similar path and now we whole heartedly approve of Sergei Rachmaninoff as a subject. In fact we are delighted with the pick." John sounded as if he meant it and Robert had no doubts he did.

Robert continued with, "I am close to having my approach visualized and if I get the initial reaction I am expecting I think it will go well. I am sure he will be on pain medication and not attentive but my opening conversation will be to make sure he understands that World War II concluded with the Allies victory in both theaters and that some semblance of peace came about. If that perks his interest I want to touch on parts of his professional life and successes and then I want to move into his personal life with his wife, daughters and close friends. I think I can make this work."

"Robert you do have a gift. We concur with your plan and will set up the mechanisms to make it happen. This coming Sunday, May twenty-fourth at eight then for a visit with Sergei Rachmaninoff. Does that sound about right?"

"Perfect."

"Good. If we need to make any changes to timing and location you will know before you travel. Everything we can determine now is your request is a go so be prepared for the thirty minute visit."

"I will be ready and I am looking forward to it. Until Sunday then," Robert responded and he meant exactly what he said.

John said "Sunday," and the iPad's home screen reappeared. He thought one of these times I should try to remember what was on the screen while conversing with John.

By mid-week Robert thought he had his Rachmaninoff data pretty much lined up. His first tour in the the United States, leaving Russia as the revolution rolled on, the early successes financially, some of his compositions he was proudest of, music by others he liked to play, his memory that allowed him to play with such confidence, his friendships and his personal life. Also was the letter he co-signed in 1931 condemning the Soviet regime that caused him grief but much later Soviet recognition in 1986 and 1999. His love of cars and his fast driving. The meeting with Igor Sikorsky and his investment with him to jump start his helicopter business. Helping Nabokov,

Chekhov and many others get their careers underway. His close friendship with Vladimir Horowitz and their dueling piano performances in his home on the two Steinway Grands at parties. There was so much color and excitement in his life there must be many things Robert could touch on that would bring up good memories and hopefully some happiness before he lost his battle.

Chapter 40

Robert decided take a little time away from Rachmaninoff and finish up his sculpture. He had found a nice shaped piece of fir with an interesting bark pattern just the right size to mount the squirrels. With some adjustment they took on the look of a wild and playful chase about a tree trunk. Donald made the requested appraisal visit and liked what he saw.

"It is a great piece and all who see it will want one. It will be good in bronze. You might want to make a few changes to make it an easier cast and save you some money."

He pointed out several places where the squirrels were gripping the bark that could be built up a little and not change the look. Also by filling all the under cuts of the natural bark with clay would avoid a lot of molding and wax chasing work. He then pointed out how the mold maker would cut the legs just above ankles leaving the feet in place and the squirrels and base would be molded and cast as separate pieces.

"You can do that and it would make sure the alignments are right when the molds are made."

Robert asked him where the foundry was that he used and it turned out it was just over the hill in San

Rafael.

"Want to drive over there tomorrow? Only take a couple of hours. I'll drive as Browser will want to go." Donald offered.

"That will be great. I'll get the squirrels ready this afternoon. You wouldn't have a pair of side cutters I can borrow. I just used the cutter on my pliers to cut the wire and that will make a mess in the clay."

As usual, Donald had every tool needed to fix everything you could think of and as Robert had used hanger wire, instead of softer aluminum wire, he would need the proper side cutters. In a few hours he had the suggestions accomplished and his three pieces were boxed and ready for the foundry. The next morning he found out the reason bronze sculptures cost so much. He handed over his Visa Card and was relieved that it was accepted by the credit card machine. The total was about one half his remaining cash assets.

The ride over with Donald was a nice change for him. It started out with a little tension as Browser had to be convinced that Robert was to sit in his front passenger seat position and he was to be in the back. He managed to position his front half on the console, in an awkward sprawl, to get his head up on Roberts lap and then promptly fall asleep. The return trip was the same with good conversation allowing Robert to relax and look at the spectacular vistas that opened up along the way. This was a beautiful area of California and just a few miles away to the east and south was an enormous concentration of people. They came to visit on this side but generally went home each evening. Maybe this could be the place was his thought along with whether July would make the decision for him.

Saturday was a fine day and Robert drove north on Highway One for about fifteen miles until he found a small parking area along the beach front to pull into. Finding one of the last parking spots he parked and started a walk heading further north on the beach. In shorts, sandals and a windbreaker he did about four miles before turning back. It was a good walk and had stopped several times to have friendly conversations with others out on a nice day. The Pacific was pacific but a quick test found the water very cold. To swim in these waters you would need a wet suit.

Sunday was just like Saturday and after handing over the station to Jerry, he walked around town for a while then headed home for a light lunch. Later, he joined Donald and Diane for dinner at one of their favorite small restaurants in town. Diane had the next month free of any seminars and she was excited to get back to painting and enjoying life at home. It seemed to Robert she looked younger and prettier than ever and that maybe Donald should convince her to limit her away time. "Life is just too short," he thought.

Sunday evening had arrived and Robert was where he was supposed to be. The iPad clock was at 7:58 PM and his nerves were on end. Much more so than the previous visits had been. He was not as confident about this one as Rachmaninoff was in pretty bad shape and would be in pain and probably sedated. It could all go wrong in the first minute. 7:59 PM, then 8:00 PM.

"Hello Robert, are you ready for your visit?" came John's clear and calm greeting.

"Hello John. Yes I am. I take it the time and place

is as planned?" was Robert's prompt response which he was hoping disguised his nervousness.

"Yes. We are confident of both and when you are ready say the word."

Robert placed the ear buds in his ears, had already located the receiver/transmitter near the iPad and had the battery charger close by just in case. He took a look around the sound proof room and the odd thought that came to his mind was how would it look as a normal bedroom in a small house in Point Reyes Station. He inhaled a deep breath and continued the protocol.

"I am ready."

"Good. There should be no problems. You will have a thirty minute visit," was John's confident answer.

Chapter 41

The concentric circles and straight lines appeared on the screen and Robert stared at them. It took just enough extra time that he noticed but before he could process that thought he was standing in a 1940's style carpeted bedroom with period furniture and a double bed with head and foot boards. In the bed was a very tall man breathing in a raspy and slightly rapid rhythm. Robert could see it was Rachmaninoff but he looked drawn and his skin was both pale and sickly looking. Robert was afraid this was not going to go well when Rachmaninoff raised his head and rasped out, "Who are you?"

"Mr. Rachmaninoff, my name is Robert Johnson and I am visiting you from seventy-two years in the future."

"You're what? Is this some kind of joke? I am dying and you are from the future. Go away!" he garbled out and tried to turn away.

Robert was ready for this and continued as if nothing had been said, "Mr. Rachmaninoff, I have only thirty minutes to visit with you and I have a number of things you would like to know before you pass." Robert paused and then continued, "Adolf Hitler committed suicide April 30, 1945. Germany signed an unconditional surrender on

May seventh, and the Japanese did likewise on September second.   World War Two was over."

Again Robert paused and then Rachmaninoff moved his head back up and tried to focus on him. When he finally made eye contact he actually hinted at a smile and said "I think I may want to hear more, Robert Johnson from seventy-two years in the future. That would be the year 2015, wouldn't it be?"

"Yes sir, Mr. Rachmaninoff, that is exactly when."

"Well let us get started but first you call me Rach! Okay, Robert?"

Robert knew he had made the breakthrough and he started conversation as planned.

"Rach, first understand you won't be remembering much of this conversation tomorrow so just concentrate on getting some pleasure on what I will tell you about what has happened involving you and your music. Also on a number of the things during your life that will be enjoyable and that we can talk about. I will start with my year today, 2015. If you could look at the play list for all the major symphonies in the United States for this season there is one name that appears on almost every one, Rachmaninoff. *Piano Concerto Number One, Number Two, Number Three, Symphonic Dances, Rhapsody on a Theme of Paganini*, the chorale pieces *The Bells* and the *Vespers*, and on and on it goes. You are one of most popular composers in the country now and have been for years."

Robert waited but Rach just stared at him. Just as he thought he should make another try Rach got out, "You mean that. It is true. You would never tell a dying man anything that is not the truth."

'It is the absolute truth, Rach. You are still a star in

2015." Robert paused and then continued, "Here is something else you would like to know. In 1986 the Moscow Conservatory dedicated a two hundred and forty-two seat auditorium to you, Rachmaninoff Hall. And in 1999 in the small town Veliky Novgorod they unveiled a monument to you, claiming their town your birth place. You are back in Russian's good will and they have claimed you as their own since the early 1980s."

"Robert you are winning me over. Tell me more. The good things. I don't have time for the bad."

"How about this long quote, Rach, 'His works have stood the test of time, and while some of his works are more fully realized than others, it is now plain to see why the best of them have won, and earned, a permanent place in the hearts of listeners everywhere'."

Rachmaninoff was quiet but Robert could see he was moved. Even a tear slid down his check.

"That was nice," he responded barely able to speak.

"Okay Rach, let me get serious here for a minute. Here is another quote 'He is six foot six inches of Russian gloom'."

This time there was an attempt at a chuckle. Robert felt he was on track and asked "How tall are you?"

"Six foot two. At least I used to be," was the quick reply. "And about that gloom comment. I don't know why it was so hard for me to smile in public, or when photographed or when playing in concert. I had a time when I was depressed and unhappy, but that was a long time ago. I have been happy most of my life. Satisfied. I didn't mean to scowl. I just did."

"Rach there are many books, photos, even movies

on your life and the ones that touch me the most are of you with your family, your wife and daughters, your friends. Those show a happy and contented man. Was it the financial drive that made you be away from what made you the happiest, or was it the music, or the need for applause and validation?" were questions Robert wanted answered but he hoped he hadn't pushed his luck.

"Robert, I won't answer that. It was all of those. That is the easy answer and you will have to be satisfied with it!" Rach spoke clearly this time and Robert knew he would have to go elsewhere.

"The story of Igor Sikorsky and you is a great one. You remember that day in 1923 when you stopped to look at the 29A?"

Rach almost smiled again. "That was a cold day. I had read a story in the paper about this Russian aeronautical genius and his plane and made the trip out to Long Island to take a look. I liked what I saw and I liked him. I knew he needed money so I wrote him a check. It was a good investment."

"It sure was. Sikorsky was the right man, in the right place at the right time. Just as you were that day. I would liked to have seen the expression on his face when you gave him the check."

"Robert, I like you." Rach choked out.

"I read a story about Igor a long time after Sikorsky was a giant company and not just a man. Can't remember who was telling it but he had called the company on business many years later and a Russian accented man answered the telephone. He asked to whom he was speaking to and it was Igor Sikorsky himself. He then asked what are you doing there and Igor answered, 'I may be 85 but this is still my company and I am here every day. If the phone rings, I answer it'."

There was another chuckle from Rach and Robert thought he looked a little better.

"Rach, I know you bought a new Cadillac every year but what was your favorite car?"

"Now you are embarrassing me. I owned so many different cars I don't remember. I can tell you that if there ever was a problem in my marriage it was about cars. Let's just say I loved them all." Rach was having a good time. At least he was able to converse and Robert was now relaxed and enjoying the moment.

"The houses and estates. How about Villa Senar on Lake Lucerne?" Robert queried.

"Villa Senar was a favorite. I did a concert in Lucerne and had a few days. A friend took me out on the lake in his fancy speedboat and we swung past this piece of property. Before I knew what I was doing I had bought it and was planning the building of the Villa with an architect. We spent a lot of time there. A beautiful place and a good place for me to work. The first item of furniture delivered was a Steinway Concert Grand Piano. You know, the big one. Also I had a dock and a fancy speedboat." Rach was now smiling. A real smile.

Robert continued the story. "I read Senar is the first two letters of Sergei and Natalya with the Rachmaninoff R at the end."

"I think you know too much, Robert."

It was Robert's turn to laugh and he rushed on "How many Steinway Grands did you own? Were they all Hamburg build or did you buy some from New York?"

"To answer your first question, I can't remember.

On the second, I started with just the Hamburg builds but later bought a number out of New York. Gave a lot of them away. There are two down stairs right now."

"Let us talk about Vladimir Horowitz. At your parties here did you two just play duets or did you have some games with each other. Like can you match this competition?"

Rach again let out a small laugh and shot back "Of course we did. Artistically we met in 1928 in Steinway Hall. He had just arrived in New York with an earned reputation as a virtuoso and we put on a show. At that time we were considered the two best pianist of our time and had a shared Russian history. We became best friends. He can play my number three better than I can. I love the man."

Robert heard the first beep and shuddered. "Rach I have only a few minutes left. Let me share just a couple of things you should know. Natalya and Irina will move back to New York. Natalya lives until 1951 and is buried next to you at Kensico Cemetery in Valhalla. Horowitz lives to old age of eighty-six and passes away in 1989. He was actively performing almost to his last day. I truly wish you had had that opportunity."

"I guess I needed to know those things. How long do I have to lay here in pain and suffering?" Rach spoke sadly.

"Six days but only four, or more accurately three. You will be unconscious the last two."

"You're an honest man, Robert. I appreciate that. This has been the best thing, this visit, that has happened since I found out I was going to die. Thank you for stopping by." It was said in a manner that left Robert thinking he had done it right.

Robert heard the three pings. He finished with "I will have to leave in a few moments. It has been an honor talking with you, Rach. I wish I had known you back then during the good times. Maybe you could have taken me for a fast drive around Beverly Hills or a speedboat ride on Lake Lucernre. I will leave you with that thought."

Robert clearly saw a smile on Rachmaninoff's face and the next second he was looking at his iPad through a thick mist of tears.

Chapter 42

The tears kept coming. Robert sat still, afraid to move. Something was not right this time. He felt deep emotions he had not had in years, if ever. He had just lost something but he couldn't think of what it was. He had told Rachmaninoff exactly what was to befall him which had seemed the right thing to do and he had accepted it without any reaction other than indicating he had wanted to know the truth. Robert's head felt strange, like it was under physical pressure as wearing a too small hat, and his eyesight was blurred. He felt weak and he didn't think he could stand without falling. He was frightened.

"Robert, stay seated for a few minutes," John's calm voice came over the ear buds. "Your vitals show your heart rate is fast and blood pressure low. You need to breath deep breaths and try to exhale as completely as possible. You have mild hypoxia and this is worrisome but should abate in fifteen minutes, or so. Keep the deep breathing until you start feeling more normal. Stay seated for at least thirty minutes. Do you understand?"

"I understand. I think so," Robert answered weakly. He was already trying to inhale and exhale with more effort as his subconscious had taken over.

"Very good, Robert. We will stay with you until

you feel comfortable." John paused and then continued "We are already seeing improvement. Keep up the deep breathing. You need all the oxygen you can get. Try to empty the lungs on each exhale. Keep up the rhythm."

Robert slowly started feeling better, his emotions seemed to come under control and the tears had stopped. He was still shaken but his focus was returning.

"Robert, your vitals are returning towards normal. Don't try to stand up yet. Do you understand?"

"Yes. I am feeling better."

"Good. That was quite a visit you had with Rachmaninoff. A very good thirty minutes. Too bad it couldn't have been longer but I assume you can see why that is the maximum we can run on one of these visits. This time it was about five minutes too long." John wanted to say more but knew this wasn't the time.

Robert solved John's thought immediately. "John, I think this will be my last visit with you. Coming back didn't go that good and it would appear these symptoms are cumulative."

"We are not going to argue the point with you as you are correct. We do want to talk with you more, both about this visit and things our group are planning in the future. Can we confer with you tomorrow night at eight?"

"Yes John. I will want to write up the visit so I trust you will send me the transcription?"

"Yes, of course we will. Robert, you did a great job again. Wonderful is more accurate. We will have a good discussion tomorrow. Try to sleep well tonight. Your vitals seem almost normal now but move carefully for the next hour. Donald and Browser are on the porch."

Robert actually had a good nights sleep. An hour

on the porch with Donald and Browser was just what he needed to bring him back to where he needed to be. Being able to tell someone about what had happened and having the unconditional love of the big dog was therapeutic. Donald was relieved that he would not be tripping back into history anymore.

Monday started as usual and Robert choose a short up hill hike after his station duties to get his system fully back. The sun coming out at mid-morning burning off the marine layer helped even more. This was a pretty place but after a simple lunch on his porch Robert began to think about his future. Did he have one and was it here? He could consider sculpture but that seemed for him more akin to a hobby than a profession. Not only did it require skill but to be successful the desire and creativity had to be there. The marketing and selling was so important and he doubted those things were in his DNA. He had no doubt he could pursue it but he really didn't think he had the needed desire to be a success. Becoming a writer had more appeal. What could be a higher calling than making a living by placing your thoughts on paper in a way that had enough value, or entertainment content, to make a living. But again, did he have the right stuff to accomplish it at a level to be successful? He had no idea but he really enjoyed putting together the visit manuscripts. They flowed almost effortlessly from his mind to the paper. Maybe?

He was sure that going back into the high tech world of engineering wasn't something he wanted to do, at least not yet. The interesting and challenging work had too much pressure, and with the possibility of it's failure or rapid obsolescence, didn't sit well with him. It could be financially rewarding but also could suddenly leave you broke and lonely. He reminisced of his last period with Engstrum Technologies. What a high that had been when it was thought the needed break through was at their fingertips. They had been so sure it would work and then just as success seemed certain a fatal flaw was discovered and it fell apart almost overnight. All that work and energy resulting in no value. It had been that big of a flaw that none of their effort could be salvaged.

That lead him to thinking of Sandra and her part of making that period the best of his life and her leaving him even more devastating than the collapse of Engstrum Technologies. He closed his eyes and could clearly see her face and smile. Almost smell her scent and feel the contours of her body. The last two weeks had started to ameliorate the pain but it now came back in full force. He descended into a place he didn't want to be.

He heard a woman say "Hi Robert. You awake up there?"

Robert tried to let the thoughts of Sandra leave and opened his eyes squinting in the direction of the voice. It was Julie Gallager.

"Hello Julie. What's up?"

Julie smiled and asked if he had time to chat a bit. He acknowledged he did and invited her to have a seat.

"You are looking pretty comfortable up here. It's a nice porch, isn't it?" was her cheerful introduction to something coming that Robert was now uncertain and uneasy about.

"It is a nice place to spend a little of one's time," Robert answered.

"Robert, Jerry asked me to talk to you as he didn't

want to do it. He doesn't like to deal with anything that might be difficult to explain or may cause someone problems. It is simply that we may be getting an offer on the house. It hasn't been for sale and we haven't even been thinking about selling it. We have a local lawyer that does our legal work and does our taxes. He is a CPA too so it just makes it easy to combine the work."

Julie paused to let Robert process this and then continued, "He was contacted and there was a very brief conversation that he thought was a bit odd. The amount being discussed was above the current market value by about ten percent. It is a lot of money. More than we anticipated. We are thinking about retirement and if this is a valid offer we may want to take it. We hope you understand."

"Of course I understand. If it works out take it. Is your lawyer competent in real estate deals? Maybe that's not any of my business but there are a lot sleazy people out there and you need to be extra careful here in California," Robert was quick to answer.

"I knew you would say that and our lawyer already said he will get help on this if it comes about. He was uncomfortable with the conversation and had some suspicions about it."

"Julie, that's good to know. Now as for me there is no problem. I was just now sitting on this nice porch trying to plan the rest of my life and I need a catalyst to get me going. If I lose my little house just two blocks from work it may just be what is needed." Robert even sounded as if was ready to move on immediately but he didn't speak to what he really wanted. That was to have a place where Sandra would want to live by his side.

Chapter 43

That evening he was sitting in front of his iPad as 8:00 PM approached and when it did the familiar, "Hello Robert," announced John's greeting.

"Hello John," Robert answered back.

"Your are feeling better I trust?"

"Yes I am. In fact, pretty good."

"Good. The transcript of your Rachmaninoff visit should be in your Email. It was such a good visit. We all went over it twice. Excellent, Robert. Excellent."

Robert waited as he knew what was coming next. At least he thought he knew.

John continued, "Robert, I want to tell you a little more about us. Not who we are or where we are located. Just what we are about. There are six of us that fully know and understand what we are trying to accomplish. We are all scientists with various specialties. Working for us are a group about twenty engineers, chemists, technicians, and others with special talents. None of them have any knowledge or understanding of what we six have been doing or want to do."

He then continued, "The project to visit history as it was happening was one of the desired pursuits of our group. The technology to do this took five years to develop and I will not tell you anything about how it is done. Each of us have made one trip to a site just making contact enough to verify the possibilities. I will tell you nothing more on this part."

Again John paused. "You have been our only traveler. You were selected for a variety of reasons, most should be obvious to you. You are smart and intelligent, which we all know are not the same thing. You had lost just about everything in the collapse of Engstrum Technologies. You went to a place that was right for what we needed for a location and circumstance played right into our hands to set things up. We were following you from your last day at Engstrum. The preparation of the sound proof room ahead of time was a gamble but the odds were good enough to have it installed. Gallager's need for an employee was known by us and your penchant to take less traveled roads, especially north of San Francisco along the coast, made Point Reyes Station a good bet. We were willing take the one in a hundred odds."

"I was the only traveler?" Robert asked with surprise in his voice.

"Yes. There was risk. Some to you but more to history. I won't elaborate on this. You handled everything correctly and not once did you even approach our emergency recall point. I won't elaborate on that either," was John's answer.

Robert came back with, "I don't want to know!"

"We didn't think you would."

"Well what happens now?" Robert questioned.

"This maybe be an interesting answer for you. First we are terminating our visit in history program. You have done so well for us that the answers we sought on a technology of this type were all answered. That is much more valuable to us than you can imagine. This brings us to the next question. How would you like to work with us on other projects? Before you answer there are some conditions that you may find unacceptable. You will not be an employee. You will not receive any direct compensation. You will not discuss anything about us unless you have our permission. And there may be other conditions that are specific to the program you may be involved with. We don't need an answer today."

Robert sat very still. This had caught him totally off guard. He then slowly offered, "I will think about it."

"That will be fine. What we would like now is for you to prepare a Sergei Rachmaninoff manuscript for us. Could you then prepare a synopsis in a way of a fictional story of each of these three visits, and propose other possible visits, such that we are able to market it as a TV series. The subject would be the visits, not your story, please understand. That you would be compensated for by a production company with no ties to us."

Robert smiled. "I may be very interested in doing something along that line."

"That is a lot to think about. A week from today we can talk some more. Monday evening at eight. Is that okay with you? Make note that it is the first of June and July is coming soon, Robert. We would like you to be with us by August."

Robert was speechless. He stuttered out "Next Monday at eight."

John was gone.

Robert was still in front of his iPad a half hour later. "What is this about the first of June and July is coming soon? Does John know everything that is going on in my life?" he said out loud and then to himself "One in a hundred chance?" A shudder coursed down his spine. "Can they be controlling my life? Is everything I am doing being run by six people in a room somewhere? Was Sandra just one part of this?" Robert questions were rattling around in his brain and he started shaking. "No! No! No! That can't be."

He jumped up and headed outside. He walked into town and then to the outskirts and into the darkness. After about a mile he stopped and looked up at the sky. It was a blaze with stars and he could name a number of them. Three constellations he recognized looked so distinct he thought they were within his grasp. "No! Nothing that was this beautiful could exist in a universe that would harbor beings that could control another man's life. What had happened had happened and John and his people were just observers who could take advantage of what they saw. They could observe. They could deduce. They could act. But they could not control his responses to his own observations and deductions."

He didn't sleep well that night. Sleep found him dreaming frustrating scenarios and waking in cold sweats. He repeated the same sequence three times until it was time to get up. He hoped his day today would be an easy one. It was and after lunch on the porch he leaned back and took a half hour nap.

Chapter 44

Robert was feeling much better after his nap and decided to download the transcript of the Rachmaninoff visit. It, like the previous two, was laid out in a way that filling in his recollections would be easy and the story of *A VISIT WITH SERGEI RACHMANINOFF* could be done in the next few days. It was and he thought it was a good story and he was happy with what he had done. The thought of wanting to make another visit back into history flashed through his mind and was quickly dismissed when remembering the problems he had upon the last return. It scared him to just think about how he felt the loss of control and fearing it wouldn't come back. Never again would he ever do such a thing.

Later in the week Donald invited Robert to do some trap shooting. It was a beautiful afternoon and the four of them, Diane and Browser the additions, headed out to the grounds. Robert had never handled a shotgun, or for that matter any gun, so the first lesson was gun safety and the protocol of shooting. As was expected, Donald was a very good and patient instructor. He and Diane each had their own shotguns, beautiful guns in hard cases, which they handled like cherished heirlooms. Robert would shoot with one of their spares but it was also a quality gun.

Donald had Robert shoot a few shots at a still target about thirty yards away and after five tries he was able to hit the center circle with the center of the shot pattern. He then explained how the clays would be launched and the calls made. Demonstrating, he shot ten for ten with such ease Robert thought that this couldn't be that hard. Diane followed with ten of ten and it was now Robert's turn. Zero for ten had him rethink how easy this would be.

The afternoon flew by and after Donald and Diane had shot hundred clays each, missing only seven between them and Robert stopping after fifty when he finally hit his first one, the day was declared a success. Browser was not recognizable to Robert, standing on point and looking at Donald after every shot. The only time he relaxed was when Robert shot. He would then lay down and take a quick snooze. Robert knew where he was placed in Browser's estimation of a bird hunter.

On the weekend Robert agreed to man the station so Jerry and Julie could have a mini-vacation. It was busy, but doable, and kept Robert from thinking about his future. By Monday afternoon he was ready to talk to John.

At 8:00 PM he was seated in front of his iPad and "Hello Robert," was almost sung out by John.

"Hello John," was promptly returned.

"As was expected we loved your manuscript on the Rachmaninoff visit. Robert, you have a way with words, you should capitalize on that. We will talk about that in a moment. First, how are you feeling, your health that is?" John's speech was still upbeat and Robert wasn't sure whether he should be pleased or wary.

"I am good and feeling fine. That was a bit scary

on the return but I am not going to forget how I felt those first two hours and I don't want to go back there." Robert was calm and felt sure he had answered several of John's questions, both the one asked and the implied ones.

"Understood and anticipated. Good. Have you given thought to doing some work for us in the future?" John responded positively.

"You have me intrigued on what I might be able to do for your team under the conditions you mentioned. At the top of the list is the idea of writing, and especially doing a TV series on the genre of the visits. That is something I would like doing. Will there be more later?" Robert came back quickly with no hesitation.

John came back just as quickly with "Great. We were planning on this and have already made contact with a producer who is interested. We will pass on *RACH-MANINOFF* today and I think we can make a deal. Have we your okay to go ahead? It will be good for you financially."

"Tell me more, John."

"We don't have the final numbers yet but as I said before you would be dealing with the producer directly and we would have no further involvement with the project. Understand we would act as your agent but as soon as the contract is signed you will have to act in your own self interest. Be assured, however, that we will serve and protect your interest on this in a way that you might guess we can do. As far as compensation let's just toss out a five figure per episode with a six episode minimum." John sounded about as excited as Robert was getting.

"Do you mean I would have three episodes about ready to be in the can, so to speak? Robert was able to get out without choking.

"Yes"

"I'm in."

"Okay Robert, we will continue with this and I think it will work out very good for you. We have more of course." John was almost giddy and continued "We would like to establish some kind of retainer for your services in the future. Let's not talk specifics or money just yet but think in terms of both our and your future. We have plans that you will not have any part in directly but we do think we will be needing help in public relations once we try to capitalize on our efforts. A lot of that will require written documentation in understandable context. You would be ideal. At that point you would become part of our team. Probably not in the group of six but as part of a new company. It will be worth your while and by that time we think you will have your financial and personal interests taken care of. Would you be interested in a proposal of this nature?"

"That is something for me to think about but the quick answer is yes!" Robert responded. Then continued, "About my personal interests. What do you know that I don't know?"

"We will only venture an educated guess but that Sandra will be coming back into your life. Whether that works out or not we have no idea. That will be up to the two of you and you both have some hurdles to clear. Robert, before we picked you for our visitor we had to examine your life in detail. I mean in detail. Sandra was such a major factor in the final choosing that we had to give her equal scrutiny. We are certain by August you will have clarity. That is all we can offer you on the subject."

At this point Robert had to take a step back. Everything sounded almost to good to be true and everyone knows the rest of that train of thought. Sandra being involved in such an open way was disturbing. His long pause caused John to respond.

"Robert, are you still with us?"

"Yes. I accept the offers and their conditions. Sandra in my life is such a big part of how I want my future to turn out that to think of that as a question makes it hard to commit entirely. The visit stories are a one hundred percent yes, the idea of the retainer and possibly joining your group has a contingency on how Sandra and I work out our relationship. Can I leave it at that?"

"Robert, we can do that. We will now establish contact via email. It will be a reply only at first and as things progress we can set up a two way contact protocol both audio and text. We will be having a lot of contact shortly and we think this is going to be a very good relationship and very good for you. Until later."

Chapter 45

The next week seemed to slip by quickly and Robert's routine became rote. Working at the station each morning. A walk around town, often stopping by the Thrift Shop making sure he didn't miss any great buys, and talking to locals whenever paths crossed. His afternoon time was spent putting together a list of visits which would fit the genre of a TV series and doing initial research on them. Then were the almost every other day walks and runs of a more athletic nature both on the beaches and in the hills. One evening after a particular rigorous run, as he was taking a shower, Robert took a close look at his body. How had this happened he thought as his now flat stomach was faintly defined by a six-pack of abdominal muscle. A closer look in the mirror made him realize he hadn't looked as good as this since he was twenty. It was a good feeling to be physically fit and he had hopes his mental fitness was catching up.

On Monday, the eighth of June, he had been doing some research on the internet and in the late afternoon he clicked on the AIS site and found *Du-eT* in Shoal Bay at the dock. Google Earth showed it to be in a nice place. Sandra and Conrad appeared to be making progress toward Alaska in the last week but it was still a long way and Robert thought to get just to Ketchikan and return to San Francisco did not match up with July, or even August. Whatever, he had gotten to the point that he could think of them together without sinking into depression. His conversation with John stayed with him and he would let that guide his thinking.

The real surprise happened the next day when he checked his email and in his inbox was mail from Chase Bank with the last four digits of his credit card exposed. He wasn't sure he wanted to open it as what other than bad news could there be waiting for him. Touching the box up popped the Chase Account Sign-In which he did. His meager Savings and Checking balances look as meager as usual. Then in the Credit Card box was a deposit notice. $10,000 was deposited on June 5, 2015. Touching the DEPOSIT button gave the date again, "Gift From Friend", and the amount.

Ten thousand dollars looked really big to someone who was down to less than a thousand. It could only come from one place so he was sure his friends, John and company, had something going for him that was going to eventually pay them back. He would ask no questions and the cushion was something he badly needed. June was starting off particularly good. "Don't get too cocky. You know better then to count your chickens before they hatch," Robert saying this out loud looked about as he was on the porch. There was no one in sight so he said it out loud again with a smile on his face.

The rest of the week was again routine. In fact Robert was starting to get restless. He didn't think he should put too much effort into his writing until he had more direction from John as to the viability of the project.

Donald had a busy schedule with several commissions to finish and it seemed that Browser was much more enthusiastic when Donald was present. Robert didn't want to analyze that behavior because Browser was a dog. Towards the end of the week the AIS showed *Du-eT* in Lagoon Cove, again at a nice marina with good docks. They seemed to be in no hurry and he was starting to think that maybe the plans of getting to Alaska had been changed.

It was on Friday that things started to happen in a big way. Jerry and Julie came over to the house after Jerry had closed up for the day. They looked to Robert that their world had dramatically changed and he was curious to know what had occurred.

"Robert you won't believe what has happened in the last two days." Julie started the conversation and then just stopped. Jerry sat down on the steps and looked like he was lost.

"Well, are you going to tell me or should I make a guess?" Robert coaxed them.

Jerry said nothing and then Julie let it all out. "We sold the station and the little house. The new owner's two sons will run the station and they will be living in a motor home behind it. For now, and for at least six months, you can live in the house as a caretaker rent free. The closings are on Tuesday, June thirtieth and it is a cash deal and we are going to retire." Julie had to stop to take a breath. Jerry just sat there with a dazed look on his face.

Robert looked over at Jerry and he thought he saw smile. Then he turned his attention to Julie and he was afraid she was going to faint.

"Whoa, you two. Let's sit down talk this over one thing at a time."

Jerry looked up at Robert and manage to get out, "Yep."

Robert went into the house and brought out another chair and they sat in a circle. Julie's opening statement was discussed one item at a time and slowly the picture unfolded. It had started a couple of weeks ago when their lawyer told them he had been approached by a potential buyer for the house. That was when Julie had come over to tell Robert about it so he would know it might happen. Their lawyer asked a real estate lawyer to help him if it came about. Last week the offer was made for both the house and the station at quite a bit more than they had thought they could ever get and the early closing was requested. A very big, non-refundable earnest money check was deposited this morning, cleared, and the papers were signed this afternoon. Both lawyers approved and were satisfied there were no problems. The buyer was paying in full and provided proof of funds. They were both in shock.

"Congratulations, you two. You have earned it and you had best just get to the first of July before you even try to think about what you should do next. Once the money is in the bank you can take a very slow and deliberate look at how to invest the funds and think about what you would like to do as a retired couple. Plan to spend some time to adjust to having the free time. It is not easy. Take your time." Robert hoped his advice was taken with the good intentions he meant.

"Robert, the free rent is odd, don't you think? Rents are pretty high here. Why would he do that?" Julie asked.

"I will have to think about this. We will see if it actually turns out that way. Did either of you speak to the lawyers about having a renter?" Both Julie and Jerry shook their heads no. Robert had a sneaking suspicion that something was going on with a group of six he may eventually be working with.

Chapter 46

Over the week-end Robert's days were somewhat boring. Other than the community table at the Bakery and the customers at the station he talked to no one. Even the sticky bun didn't seem to be quite as good as usual. Not hearing from John yet was a bother to him as he was ready to get started on the writing. He had a number of ways to develop the traveler's lead into the visits. It would be based on similar circumstances as his own but enough different in sequence and location to make it total fiction. He could use his own experiences and thoughts as the events unfolded to make it all seem real. What he needed was the go ahead.

Robert was now checking his email twice a day and almost as often the progress of *Du-eT* on the AIS site. They had made a move to Sullivan Bay and stayed there three days. This was about the place they would have to get into more open water and into the ferry routes to Port Rupert and on to Ketchikan. Their next port was Port Mc-Neil. This appeared to Robert to be going the wrong direction as Port Hardy looked like it would be the logical one to leave from towards Prince Rupert. Mid-day on the eighteenth they were headed south down the Johnstone Strait. Their plans had changed and Robert couldn't help but think something was wrong. That night they were at April Point Marina, just across from Campbell River, at the dock. It must have been a long, stressful day. He wished Sandra would send him an Email.

Saturday, June 20, 2015 was a day Robert would remember the rest of his life. He had opened the station and was home by ten-thirty. He was going for one of his more testing runs after a light lunch and a short rest. He opened his home page on the iPad and mail showed two new emails. A click and the first one was from John. It was short and sweet. "We have a deal on the TV series. You will be contacted in about two weeks. They are in San Francisco. You will like it. Congratulations. John." It was a no reply mail. Robert just smiled and thought "My world has just gotten more interesting."

He then tapped the second email and his world got much more complicated. It was from Sandra and was likewise short but not sweet. "Robert, I need help. Please email me back. Conrad is in the hospital and is not expected to live. Sandra." This time Robert thought his world had just turned upside down.

Thinking clearly was going to be difficult and it was. He had two weeks to clear to out help Sandra and that was his only priority. If need be he would just postpone, or give up, the television deal. Sandra came first no matter how it may turn out.

He replied with volunteering what ever was needed. He could buy one of those short term mobile telephones and send her the number. If she had a contact phone number to email it to him and he would call her. He could leave immediately and be there tomorrow night or early the next morning. What ever you need. He composed the reply and hit the send button. And then waited.

Two hours later Sandra answered. Again she was brief. She would explain everything when she saw him but for him to be with her right now was what she needed most. There was so much involved in the hospital arrangements, what to do for Conrad, the boat and how to get it back to San Francisco and how to pay for it all was overwhelming her. She ended the email with "You are the only person I know I can ask for help. Please come as soon as possible. Please, Robert. Sandra." Robert would be leaving in an hour. It was eleven hundred miles and a twenty-three to twenty-eight hour drive depending on one ferry crossing and customs. He could get there tomorrow night late but would for sure make it early Monday morning. His reply told her that and he hoped a lot more.

Robert did his best. He touched base with Donald and Diane and they both wished him well. He filled up the gas tank, told Jerry his plans, apologized for such short notice and that it could be a week, or more, before he would be back. He left Point Reyes Station around two-thirty and arrived in Campbell River early Monday, exhausted. He went to the hospital first and checked on Conrad's condition. All he was told was that his condition remained the same. He inquired of one of the nurses about Sandra Williams and she responded with, "That poor woman. I don't think I have ever seen a lady in such distress. Such a pretty lady to be so sad."

"Do you know where she is staying?"

"I think she is on their boat at April Point Marina. She takes the water taxi back and forth and it runs every hour this time of year. You could wait here as I expect her any minute." the nurse responded.

Robert thanked her and went outside. It was a gloomy morning and chilly. He found a bench near the entrance with a view out over the water. Ignoring the cars and other buildings the scenery was nice. Blue water, green trees and, if you had an imagination, snow capped mountain in the distance. It was then another sight came into view and Robert's eyes filled with tears.

Sandra ran up to Robert, putting her arms around him in a tight embrace, and was crying so hard that nothing could be said. It was several minutes before a word was spoken. Robert had kissed her tear streaked cheeks and they leaned back and looked at each other. Sandra said "Thank you Robert, thank you, thank you."

"I want more than anything to be here. You must know that. I want to be here. Let's find a place to talk. Tell me what has happened and we will figure out what to do. The nurse only told me Conrad's condition was unchanged." Robert managed to sound calm but he was choked up with an emotion he could barely control.

They found a deserted waiting room and sat close together. Sandra had lost weight and looked haggard but was still beautiful to Robert. Deep dark circles under her eyes showed stress and lack of sleep.

"You don't have to do any explaining to me right now but tell me what has happened to Conrad and what you need," Robert whispered in her ear. Sandra had started sobbing again and he wrapped her up in his arms and waited.

Finally she started her story. "Conrad has pancreatic cancer. It was diagnosed right after the company folded and just after he bought *Du-eT*. The prognosis was for up to a year but there was no cure. It was too far along and although they might be able to give him some extra time his quality of life would be so poor it wasn't deemed worth it." She paused, a few more tears ran down her cheeks, and then she continued. "His original idea was to sail around the world. He was going to hire a two man crew and go for as long as it took. The cancer diagnosis shortened it to this trip. He also decided against a crew and there is more to that than I want to talk about right now."

"I don't need to know anything about that. I liked Conrad and I'll remember him that way."

"Robert you have to know I knew about his homosexuality months ago and that didn't bother me at all. I have to tell you I wouldn't have gone with him if he had been straight. I liked him, just like you did, as a person and it was near to a father daughter relationship. He treated me so nice. I can't tell how good a time we had together on that basis." The tears came again and Robert thought they might never stop. Eventually they did.

"He has only a few days left according to the doctors. He was feeling good until about two weeks ago. He went downhill fast. I could see the life leaving him. His appetite left him. He stopped talking to me except when I asked him a direct question. When we left Lagoon Cove he totally lost interest in where we were. He got up every morning, dressed and sat in the cock-pit while I ran the boat but showed no interest in where we were. We stayed extra nights in several marinas but he did not change. At Sullivan Bay he looked at me and said 'We better head home.' When we got here and he didn't get up the next morning I called the Medics."

Chapter 47

They had an adequate hospital meal for dinner that night. Both were exhausted and emotionally drained. Robert asked Sandra where she was staying and she told him on the boat. It was their first awkward moment. She looked at him for a long moment and then carefully approached the subject they both knew was coming.

"Robert you can come with me. There is plenty of room on the boat and I don't want to be alone. But I am not ready to have a relationship with you now, or with anyone, and it may be some time before I even want to think about having one. I just don't want to be alone." Her eyes were welling up with tears but they didn't fall.

"I understand. I promise there will be no pressure put on you. I do want to have the chance to see if we can make another start at sometime in the future. After we get things straightened out with Conrad, the boat, get you back to a place you can find some happiness, I want for us to try for what we had before." As Robert said this he was trying to hide his emotions but it wasn't working.

"I can live with that. Let's give us some time. I need some time to sort things out about myself and what I have done. There should be a water taxi in about fifteen minutes."

They were back to the boat in a half hour. Robert had never been on a sailboat before. The Tartan 4700 is a beautiful one and as he looked around he could feel it's magic. His first thought was that he may have missed something he might have loved doing. The sight of Sandra moving about the deck, and below in the softly lit cabin, forced him to promise himself to keep the promise he had made to her. It was going to be difficult.

Sandra said she couldn't use the aft cabin as that was Conrad's and she slept in the forward one. There was a crew cabin just forward of mid ship on the starboard side but it's bunk was just six feet and he might find making up the cushions that can be arranged on the lowered salon table more comfortable. They readied to retire and had settled in by ten. An hour later Sandra came to Robert and slid in next to him. "Hold me, Robert. Please, just hold me," and her tears came again. Sleep eventually came for her but Robert slept only in the hour just before the sun came up.

When they got to the hospital the charge nurse greeted them with the news that Conrad was not expected to make it through the day. He remained unconscious and his vital signs were weakening. There was no sense in doing anymore for him. They went to his room and Sandra sat next to him. She kissed his forehead and then held his hand until he stopped breathing. A doctor came in and felt for a pulse, the monitors having flat lined, and pronounced his death.

At 2:37 PM Conrad Engstrum died. June 23, 2015 at the age of sixty-seven. Sandra and Robert would later compose his obituary but found they actually knew very little about him. It was disheartening that that was the case. His passport said he was born on February 5, 1948 in Prescott, Arizona. Other than all the stories about Engstrum Technologies the internet had no other information about him. It was almost as if he hadn't existed before his start up had been funded and then it's collapse. The obituary was short and very personal.

One of the hospital administers found them outside Conrad's room and started the conversation on how they planned to have Conrad's body tended. The hospital had a mortuary where the medical examiner would process the death certificate and they would hold the body for twenty-four hours after which charges would be imposed. He asked if he had left a will and instructions in case of death. Sandra offered that she didn't know and they hadn't discussed it. Conrad was a very thorough man and she thought there may be papers on the boat. She and Robert would go and see if they could find them.

It was already late afternoon by the time they were back on board. Sandra asked Robert if he would do the search as she didn't want to go through Conrad's things. It bothered her just thinking about doing it. He did and it only took ten minutes to find a zippered leather case the size of a large business letter envelop. Inside was a will, instruction for care of his remains if it became necessary and a number of other papers of legal and insurance nature. Robert just made a quick survey and brought them up to the salon.

"There are a lot of papers here. We should probably find an attorney to go through them and give us some advice." Robert suggested. Sandra was tiring and Robert was almost numb with fatigue. It was getting late so they decided to wait until tomorrow to make arrangements at the hospital.

"Do you have a telephone?"

"Conrad's is here somewhere." Sandra started sifting among some things on the chart table and came up with a fancy iPhone. Robert called the number the administrator had given him and it was answered immediately. The short conversation was that tomorrow morning would be fine and he could recommend a local attorney to help them go through the paper work.

"Sandra what do you want to do with the boat?"

She looked at Robert for a brief moment thinking about the question. Then answered "I think we should get it back to San Francisco and decide what to do then. I don't want to take it down myself so I guess we should hire a delivery captain."

"I met one in Point Reyes that has done a number runs both up and down. He had just dropped off a boat in Anacortes for a customer and was headed home in a one way rental car. He had stopped in for dinner when I was at the community table. I liked him."

"Robert we are only two days from Anacortes if we don't do tourist things. Three days max. Call him and see if he could take it down." Sandra sounded ready to get this decision made and off her shoulders.

Robert fished out Captain Alan Parson's card and dialed his number. Captain Alan answered and the question was asked. Alan asked the name of the boat, make, year, type and length. Robert heard the keys of a computer typing away and then he came back with a surprise.

"Robert that is one fine boat. I'd love to bring her down. *Du-eT* is an odd name and the registration shows co-owners. Conrad Engstrum and Sandra Williams. Is either one available to handle the paper work?"

"Would you repeat the registration names," and Robert held out the phone towards Sandra.

"Sure. Conrad Engstrum and Sandra Williams. Are they a couple or related. Don't often see different surnames," was Captain Alan's clear voice. After a long pause he came back with, "Are you still there, Robert?"

"Yes. Just a bit of surprise that Sandra Williams is a co-owner. She didn't know about that."

"Robert, is this the same boat and couple you were talking about in Point Reyes that time?"

"Yes, but it would be best we don't bring that up right now," Robert saying this hoping Sandra wasn't paying close attention.

"Tell you what Robert, I am delivering a boat to Anacortes and plan to be there in five days with a crew mate. A turn around delivery will make our trip. Is it possible?"

Robert looked at Sandra and she smiled, the first smile he had seen so far and it melted his heart.

"Alan, we are in Campbell River and unless we have problems here we should be in Anacortes in three or four days. Plan on it unless you hear different," was Robert's answer.

"Your on, mate. See you in Anacortes." Captain Allan Parsons sounded happy.

Chapter 48

The next day was one of those times that all went as planned. The attorney the hospital administer had recommended, Alexander Fields, had time for a morning appointment at his office which was just two blocks from the hospital. He was cordial, friendly and upon quickly looking over the papers from the leather holder smiled.

"Your Mr. Engstrum has done you a big favor. He has signed, and had notarized, how his remains are to be taken care of specifying cremation and no autopsy unless it is required by law. The title on the Tartan 4700 was amended to add Sandra Williams as co-owner and is in order and as far as I can see cannot be challenged. His will is clear but has an interesting concept and should therefore be probated in a California jurisdiction. All his property, excluding the boat which legally becomes Ms. Williams on his death, is to be liquidated and the proceeds divided among his former employees of Engstrum Technologies based on the ratio of their annual salaries. He lists no known living relatives or dependents. It is all very clear and legal as far as I can determine."

Robert looked at Sandra and said "Conrad was as nice a man as we both thought. There is a lesson here one should learn. I know the failure of his company hurt him personally and he was broken hearted by having to let all of us go as he did but he had no choice because of the structure of the company. Trying to give something back as compensation is beyond the call but that was the kind of man he was."

Sandra nodded her head and Robert could see the tears forming so he quickly asked Alexander a question. "How was Sandra made a co-owner of *Du-eT* with out her knowing about it?"

"Very clever on Engstrum's part. He had her sign some papers regarding her joining him on the boat and going out to sea. Clever, as in the body of the agreement was the assignment as co-owner. Her signature was notarized, as was his, and that was all it would take as he was the sole owner at the time and there was no mortgage or loan against his ownership. Very clever indeed."

Alexander told them he would have all the paper work needed by the hospital ready and in their hands by mid-afternoon and didn't see any reason they couldn't leave the next day if they wanted. After the cremation the remains can be shipped to Sandra to be scattered as requested by Engstrum in a "pretty and peaceful place."

They thanked Alexander and paid his very modest fee. Leaving the office Sandra took Robert's hand and squeezed it tight. They walked back to the hospital holding hands.

At the hospital they spoke to the administer about their visit with the attorney, thanked him for the recommendation and told him that Fields would be providing him with all the necessary documentation to release Engstrum's body to the mortuary. They then took a cab to the mortuary and made the arrangements necessary and paid the fees. Conrad's ashes would be mailed to Robert's address in Point Reyes Station. Again, the paperwork would be provided by Fields. Everyone involved was familiar with the process of dealing with the situation of an American dying in Canada and how it was to be handled.

It was just noon and they had done all they could at the moment. Sandra seemed to Robert to have found some hope in the future and he could tell how relieved she was to get this part under control.

"Let's find an outdoor table and have lunch along the shore. We can walk back towards the hospital and when the right place shows up we will take a seat," was Robert's suggestion.

"Yes." was all Sandra said as she took Robert's hand again. They walked along the sidewalk next to the marina basin and chose a sea food place with an open table in just the right place. The sun had come out and although the air still had a chill it was warming up fast. The boats were a pleasant distraction and they had a nice hour where they could relax. Sandra caught his appreciating gaze a couple of times and managed small smiles. Robert knew what was happening to him but also knew Sandra was not there yet. It was going to take time, maybe a lot, and he was not going to jeopardize the possibilities by rushing her.

By early afternoon they had returned to the hospital and found that Alexander Fields was a man of his word and all the paper work was in order. The fee at the hospital was very reasonable and was settled with Robert's credit card. He said a silent thank you to his "Gift From A Friend." They had arranged all that needed to be done in Campbell River and everyone involved felt that they could head out in the morning. At a grocery store they purchased groceries for three days and caught the water taxi back to April Point and *Du-eT*. They were the only passengers on this trip and sat close together in silence. Sandra suddenly reached for and took Robert's hands, pulled him closer, and kissed him on the lips. "Thank you, Robert," she was able to get out before the tears started again.

Once on the boat Sandra took charge with her student hustling around after her. First was a check in the engine compartment of the oil level and a general inspection of the belts, hoses, the sump and the transmission. A check of the circuit panel in the salon and a quick look at the battery voltages. Next they went into the cockpit, Sandra starting the engine and letting it run for a few minutes. The oil pressure and water temperature gauges showed normal. A walk around the deck checking the dock lines, fenders and making sure the anchor was secure. Since they would be motoring the entire way the sails were left covered and tied in place. The dingy was checked and the cover secured.

"We are sea worthy and can leave at dawn," Sandra pronounced with confidence. It was all Robert could do to not reach for her and hold her to him. He would have to wait.

They had dinner on board and as dusk changed to night it seemed to them both that things would work out for them. Robert could tell Sandra was feeling better and she finally asked him the question he wasn't sure he could answer. It was a simple question.

"So Robert, what have you been up to since I last saw you?"

Chapter 49

Robert sat opposite Sandra in the salon with the table between them. They had shared a pastry they had bought at the grocery store for desert. That had been a mistake as it tasted just like a grocery store pastry always tasted but they ate it anyway.

Sandra looked him in the eye and said, "So?"

"There is the long story and the short story. The true story which you won't believe and the false story which you won't believe either," was Robert's attempt to start.

"Just entertain me and mix them all up. I want to know what you have been doing in Point Reyes and who you have met that you like. Why you stopped there. I want to hear your voice. Just tell me a story."

"All right, here goes. I left the apartment on the last day of the lease and turned left on Geary and without any planning had dinner at the Golden Arches in San Rafael. I drove up to that little park near there and slept in the van. The next day I stopped in Point Reyes Station to buy gas and got into a conversation with the owner. He said he needed someone to run it so he and his wife could take a cruise they had made reservations for and he didn't have anyone to cover for him yet. They were to leave in two days. If I would do it he had a little house I could stay in and I would be his best friend ever, forever. How could I refuse. I am still in the little house and open the station every morning to pay the rent. And that is my story." Robert leaned back and watched Sandra. The light in the salon was soft and when she nodded and smiled all doubt left him. This had to work out.

"That was so nice but there is more and I will make you tell me. Something, or someone, has entered your life. Are you going to tell me or make me wait?" Sandra was still smiling and so he started to tell her more.

"Just a few houses down the street lives an artist and his wife, also an artist, and their dog Browser. They are in their early sixties although you would never know it. I don't know how old Browser is but that makes no difference. We have bonded. Donald has become a good friend, and likewise Diane his wife, but Browser is different. I want you to meet the three of them. You will like them and they will like you. Now you know the ones that have entered my life. Jerry and Julie own the gas station. You will like them too. You may even like Point Reyes Station. Do you remember the Bakery and the sticky bun we shared there?"

Sandra at first smiled and then grew serious. "Yes I do remember the sticky bun. I wish I was sharing one with you right now. It was so good and I was so happy. I want to be there again Robert." She got to her feet and went into the forward cabin and closed the door. Robert heard her muffled crying and he knew he had to be patient.

In the morning, after a quick breakfast, Sandra gave Robert a lesson in dock line handling, started the engine, brought up the chart plotter and had him loosen the bow line and bring it in. She maneuvered the boat such that the bow swung out and then called for the stern line to be let loose and brought in. They were under way and about thirty minutes later were in open water heading for Anacortes. Robert had gotten the three fenders on board and looped up the two dock lines and secured them on the life lines. It was a nice and relaxed day and they were docked in Nanaimo by four o'clock. Even the docking had gone well as Robert was able to lasso both of the cleats on first his tries and tighten the lines correctly. Captain Sandra heaped praise on her neophyte crewman.

A welcomed walk along the marina's sidewalk, holding hands, was pleasant as the area was a beehive of activity and the general mood of the crowd having a good time. Dinner was on board and the shared sticky bun just purchased fresh from the small bakery rivaled the Bakery's of Point Reyes Station. They were both tired and Sandra went to her cabin and Robert fixed his place in the salon. He had trouble getting to sleep but finally the last few days and the day on the water did him in. He was still asleep when a gentle hand rubbed his shoulder. Sandra was actually smiling and told him it was time to get a move on. As he sat up she leaned in close, kissed him and then backed away.

"I'm coming back to feeling human again. I guess I lost that feeling when I left you after the closing of Conrad's company. That may have been the biggest mistake I have ever made. Maybe it wasn't, but I'm now getting back to where I want to be. Wait for me to get there."

She turned and went up on deck. An early start had them at the U. S. Customs dock in Point Roberts just before noon and although they were a bit concerned it went quickly. There was a phone used to announce your presence and within a few minutes the agent arrived, passports were checked, where you had traveled was asked and a two minute look around the boat. "Have a good day," and they were off the dock. They would get to Anacortes before dark. A walk around town was fun. A light dinner at one of the small bistros and it was time to retire. As the night before they both slept well and morning came clear and with just a slight breeze.

With the boat secured, it was now time to get back to Campbell River and pick up Robert's van. A one way car rental would be hard to get and asking advice from the dock master, which is always the first thing you should do, had good fortune waiting. A couple was just preparing to leave for home in Nanaimo in their new boat and were wishing they didn't have to come back here to pick up their car. She gave Robert the telephone and slip numbers and in an hour the arrangements were made for him to drive it up and in turn they would run them up to Campbell River. There was some minor paper work to do and they gave Robert the keys.

The owner asked, "You ever drive a Porsche 911 before?"

"Are you kidding me? You would let someone you don't even know drive your Porsche? But yes, my last car was a 911 S and I loved it," was Robert's disbelieving response.

"Well that's good, Robert. That is good. It is only a car, my man."

"Sure," thought Robert, then added, "I am a good driver and will be careful."

"Good. We are leaving tomorrow morning early,

and plan to make it in one day, so why don't you plan on day after tomorrow and I will run you two up to Campbell River in my wife's car. I have business there anyway so it's no problem. You should be able to get to Nanaimo in plenty of time to ride up there with me."

Robert said, "Should work out fine. What a break for us."

"A guy needs a good break once in a while."

With a slight delay entering Canada at customs getting off the morning ferry from Port Angeles they were in Nanaimo by two and standing next to Robert's van in Campbell River at four-fifteen. Everything went like clock work. A quick visit to the hospital and the news from the director that all was fine and that Conrad would be cremated as scheduled. Robert could feel Sandra clutching at his arm and he squeezed her hand in return. They left the parking lot forty-five minutes later and drove back down Highway 19A they had just come up. They were entering Qualicum Beach just at dusk and Robert pulled into a small motel parking area.

"Is this okay with you?" he asked as gently as he could.

"Just get one room. You promise to just hold me, nothing more?"

"Yes." and he went to the office and rented the room. They went to a nearby diner, had homemade chowder and lots of crackers. A shared ice cream cone, with a walk along the shore side path, they then headed back to the motel. Robert kept his promise.

The next morning dawned in a spectacular sun rise and with donuts and coffee from the motel they headed the longer but more scenic route which they had done going the other direction yesterday from Anacortes. As the day went on the previous trip in the Porsche 911 seemed to have gone much faster than this one in the van.

That night on the boat was a little more difficult for Robert than the night before. It was about two in the morning when Sandra snuggled into bed next to him and hugged him from behind. All she said was, "Robert," and fell asleep.

Captain Alan Parsons had arrived that night and Robert and Sandra were able to ready all the paperwork for his delivery of *Du-eT* to San Francisco. Robert used a bank ATM to give Alan half of his fee in cash which he much appreciated. He toured the boat and was smiling the whole time.

"What a beautiful boat. This is what I would want. First choice. I will treat her like my own."

He got a hug from Sandra and a hand shake from Robert.

They headed south via the scenic route joining highway 101 and driving along the Hood Canal and then to the coast and into Oregon. As night approached and they were just south of Reedsport a sign for Tugman State Park, or something like that, caught Sandra's eye. She looked at Robert and said, "Pull in here."

Robert pulled in and looked at her.

"You have an air mattress and a big blanket. I see two pillows. You can have the little one. It is time to stop isn't it?" She was smiling and Robert was now totally in love. They found a camp site and pulled into it. A quick use of the restrooms and arranging the bedding found Sandra comfortable on the air mattress and Robert willing to do anything for her. Fully clothed and tired they snuggled together with Robert holding her close. She felt so good next to him. She smelled good. It was almost overpowering. She kissed him hard and whispered, "Take me home tomorrow."

Chapter 50

They drove into Point Reyes Station about four-thirty and Robert drove straight to the little house just two blocks from the station. Parking on the driveway side they went up the three steps to the porch. Sandra looked around and came up with, "It's cute." Robert didn't know if that was a good, or not so good, opinion. He unlocked the door, opened it and they went inside. It looked different somehow and he could smell fresh paint. He turned on the lights and things were different.

"Robert, this is really nice. A nice kitchen with new appliances. Nice furniture and good layout. I like it. Why didn't you tell me how nice it is?" and she was off to the first bedroom. "It's nice but a little small. Still plenty of room for us." A peak in the bathroom elicited another rave review and she then headed for the sound proof room and Robert stood frozen, fearing what she would say when she saw it. "Oh! Robert! This is our room. It is perfect. Come here!"

Robert was now totally confused. He had been gone just twelve days but there were enough changes that he was having trouble sorting them out. When he looked into the room Sandra was standing next to a queen size bed and an all new bedroom that was perfectly done.

Fresh paint and plush carpeting. Quality furniture and two windows. There was a walk in closet that he was sure was not there before. The two windows had been covered and he couldn't remember seeing them from the outside. It was indeed a fine room.

"Robert, I was afraid I would end up in a rustic cabin with an out house but I had decided over the last week that I could live with that if I could be with you again. But this is perfect. Can we stay here a while? Can this be our home for right now?"

"I think so. This was a nice little place but this room was totally different two weeks ago." Robert couldn't think of what was going on. The new owners were supposed to close on the property yesterday. All this had to have been done before then.

"What I was told by Jerry and Julie is that the new owners said I could stay here for at least 6 months as a caretaker, rent free. It sounded a bit generous and with all these improvements it may not be still the case. They didn't change the locks. Jerry, or Julie, would have emailed me if there had been any changes about my staying here. Besides all my stuff is still here.

Sandra left the bedroom with Robert while they looked around the living area more carefully. Sandra picked up a leather bound book with gold embossed printing on the cover.

"What a beautiful book. Soft leather and so nicely titled. Visits to History as it Happened, Abraham Lincoln, November 18, 1863, Leonardo da Vinci, April 29, 1519, Sergei Rachmaninoff, March 22, 1943, by Robert Johnson." Sandra stared at the cover, then clutched the book to her breasts. "Robert, what is this?"

Robert couldn't answer. He didn't know. He walked over and stood next to her and she lowered the book so he could see the front cover but wouldn't let go of it. "What is this?" she repeated her question.

He went over to the book case and took out the three stationery binders and opened the first one. His manuscript was inside. Looking at Sandra he managed to stutter out, "I wrote three stories on visits to past history as interviews with famous people of the time. They were for some organization I don't know too much about and they must have decided they were worth binding like that. They are trying to set up a TV series with a production company in San Francisco."

"I am going to need more than that!" Sandra demanded, clutching the book back against herself and beginning a closer look about the room. "Where did you get the nice sculpture?" pointing to his squirrel sculpture on top of the bookcase.

Robert was now running out of rational thoughts. He was tired from the long drive. He hadn't slept very well on the hard van floor last night and he was totally confused on what was happening at the moment.

"Sandra, let's go for a short walk. I know a spot that has a bench where we can sit and I will try to tell what has happened. It is the story you won't believe. I think I can't think straight anymore."

Sandra could see the confusion and fatigue in Robert's eyes, put the book down and embraced him, kissing his face and lips. She spoke softly in his ear. "Let's go lay down on that nice bed and you can tell me whatever you want. We can get to the details when the time is right." and she pulled him into the bedroom.

They woke an hour later, still fully clothed and wrapped in each others arms. Sandra smiled and Robert knew this had worked out as he had hoped. Sandra shifted on the bed and said in a confident voice "Let's clean up and head to the Bakery for dinner and then take that short walk. We will then come back right here and make up for the three months of being apart. The whole story can wait. It doesn't make any difference to me what it is because this is were I want to be and you, Robert, are who I want to be here with."

Robert just smiled at her and thought that sounded perfect but his next thought was, "maybe it should be a quick dinner and a very short walk."

Chapter 51

The next morning Robert awakened first. The next few minutes were the best minutes he had ever experienced. He couldn't imagine he would ever have any as good again. Sandra was still in a sound sleep. They were laying face to face on the same pillow but not touching. He was looking directly at her closed eyes, each eyelash in sharp focus as was her entire face. The dark circles and bags under her eyes were gone, her complexion perfect again and fresh from a good night's sleep. Carefully, he moved his free hand lifting the sheet just enough to let his fingertips gently slide along her thigh and up over the curve of her hip to her waist. Just a hint of a smile came to her lips. It took his breath away as to how beautiful she looked. He held absolutely still and just watched her breathe and wished the moment could last forever. Her eyes slowly opened and then the smile she presented made his world even better.

"Well big boy, I think we made up for some of the last three months last night," and her laughter brightening his morning even more.

"I am the luckiest man on earth," Robert ventured and then added "There is nothing I can ask for that could make this moment any better."

"Oh, is that so?" was Sandra's reply and Robert's morning got even better.

Sandra took her shower first and when finished asked Robert to bring her a towel. There was a more for him as he dried her off spending considerably more time than necessary. After he showered and dressed he found Sandra in the living area standing next to the squirrel sculpture.

"Now what does the signature R. Johnson, 2015, and one slash twenty-five mean, exactly?"

"I guess that is part of the story I haven't told you yet. How about after a sticky bun, with OJ and coffee, at the Bakery we take that short walk we didn't get around to last night. I will tell you how that happened. You can believe this one." Robert felt confident about this at least and could let a genuine smile show.

"OK! It is time for the sticky bun."

Most of the locals at the community table had had their communion and the Bakery's breakfast crowd had left. When Suz showed up with Robert's usual and saw Sandra she took a double take. "Whoops, what can I bring the lady?" she asked and Robert answered the same. She scurried back to the counter and was back in thirty seconds with Sandra's orange juice, sticky bun and coffee.

Robert introduced them. Suz smiled and, half joking, told Sandra she now understood why none of the local girls, including herself, could even catch his eye. "We were afraid he was gay or, even worse, didn't care." Sandra's smile worked it's magic and Suz walked away happy for them both.

They started their walk and were about half way to the bench when Robert spotted the familiar sight of the big man and the big dog.

"Get behind me and hang on. You are about to meet Browser." Sandra did as told and had taken a good stance when Browser made his slightly late attempt to slow down and decided to halt his slide by rearing up putting his huge paws on Robert's shoulders. Robert just managed to hold his position and tried to get hold of Browser's ears for a good pull as the dogs big tongue began licking his face. Sandra's laughter was loud and excited and after the initial licking Browser realized there was someone behind Robert. He kept his position and twisted his head, neck and shoulders around so he could see who was there. Robert and Sandra both said later he smiled at her, got back on all fours, walked around Robert, and sat lifting his right paw up which Sandra then shook.

Donald Connor was then introduced to Sandra. The big man beamed his approval and an immediate friendship started. His first words to Sandra were "Robert has ruined my hunting dog. And it looks like you are having the same affect on him."

After some more conversation Donald and Browser, tail wagging, headed on their path home. Going in the opposite direction Robert and Sandra, holding hands, walked along not talking much but both loving life and each other. When they reached the bench they sat close together and Robert started his story on how the sculpture ended up on his bookcase.

"About seven weeks ago Donald asked me if I could help him finish a commissioned sculpture. He was running behind and it needed some detail finish work done that he thought I might be able to handle. It turned out I could and then he encouraged me to try doing a sculpture of my own. He set me up with the tools and clay and showed me the basics. He was actually a bit annoyed when the little squirrels came out so good. He insisted I have a mold made and a casting done. Took me to the foundry he uses, made the introduction, set up the casting schedule and apparently saw it got finished and put number one on the bookcase. That was really fast service, maybe because I paid in full up front. That is what happened."

Sandra listened and was rubbing his back. He was glad she was listening and he was enjoying the back rub. "That was your first sculpture?"

"Yes. I did a lot of feather details on Donald's swan but that is my first piece."

"Do you want to do more? Make a living at sculpturing?" Sandra asked, in a somewhat doubtful tone.

"I don't think so. Maybe as a hobby or part time. It is so expensive to cast bronzes and it takes a good sales personality to be successful professionally. Wait until you see Donald's watercolors. You won't believe how good they are."

They sat a while longer then headed back. Sandra was quiet for a while and then said, "Okay, one story told and accepted. By this time tomorrow I want to hear how you visited history as it was happening."

"We will work on that together. Read the first story on Lincoln in the fancy book and I will tell you exactly what happened. You won't believe it. What scares me, beyond words, is that we wouldn't be here together if it hadn't. I don't even want to think of that." He turned to her and held her as tight as he dared and she could feel him shaking.

That afternoon they made their first trip to the market together and stocked up the pantry. Sandra knew the ropes and Robert pushed the grocery cart. They made a good team. A tenderloin steak was a special treat for tonight's dinner at home. It was Sandra's new home and she knew how to make it one for Robert.

Chapter 52

Robert and Sandra unloaded the van and the bags of groceries covered every flat space in the kitchen. In the three months Robert had lived in the house there was never more than a day or two of food stored. The condiments and spices consisted of a bottle of ketchup and two small shakers with salt and pepper. Sandra told Robert to leave her space and she would take care of the kitchen. Robert thought that a very good idea, picked up his iPad and headed for the porch.

It had been some time since he had checked his email. He thought it had been since he used the hospital Wi-Fi in Campbell River. It seemed a lifetime ago. So much had happened since he first saw Sandra walking towards him that first morning he waited outside the hospital. It was a blur and now here he sat on the porch of the little house where his life had changed. He was now the happiest he had ever been. He forced himself to stay put in the chair on the porch and not go back into the house to make sure he wasn't just dreaming that she was there.

He brought up the home page on his iPad and touched the mail icon. The Inbox had two new messages. One he recognized as from John and the other was from Captain Alan Parsons. He opened Alan's first. It was from his iPhone and described their great run out of Anacortes on the out going tidal surge and a fast two days with the south current and westerly winds making for great sailing. They expected to be going under the Golden Gate at sunrise tomorrow and should be at the dock rented by the boat broker Conrad had purchased it through around eight. He listed all the particulars including the brokers name and telephone number. They could meet when he and Sandra next came over to San Francisco.

He then tapped John's email and the message was short and had been sent just the day before. It read he would be using a different email address from now on for corresponding. You can reply and it is open channel. Look for it in Junk Email under John. It was there and Robert brought it up. It was brief but informative and more personal. John wrote that he hoped the house pleased Sandra and he was glad all had worked out for them. He also noted that he was pleased that Robert's life was in a better place. The TV series was progressing nicely. The Lincoln visit had been converted into a screen writer's format and they were in the early planning with the staging and costume design. The producers would like to meet with him as soon as possible in San Francisco. His group would provide him with an agent. The names and telephone numbers were there. Finally he suggested that he bring Sandra to the meeting.

Robert sat back and thought about that last sentence. He wasn't going anywhere, or would be doing anything, without her. But everything he had done with this John and his group had him thinking they knew more about him than he did. Did they know as much about Sandra? She would be with him regardless but the thought was tucked away in his brain and wasn't likely to go away.

He moved John's and Alan's letters to the Inbox and then printed copies of both using the Wi-Fi printer feature. He went in to check on the print outs and saw Sandra busy in the kitchen with half of their supplies still awaiting their place. He walked up behind her and put his arm around her waist. She turned to face him and she looked so happy he could only smile. She kissed him. It was a good kiss, with the promise of many more to come. She told him to return to the porch and that she would be done in an half hour. He did what he was told.

Robert sat and looked about. It was a short street, only a few blocks long, and the homes were for the most case modest. His view off the porch was of other porches but raising your gaze over the roof tops the pacific hills and mountains gave you a feeling of being away from everything. It was a short walk to have that feeling become a reality. That was something he was beginning to realize was of true value. He was hoping Sandra would discover it on her own.

The next thing he sensed was her making herself comfortable in her chair with the the big leather visit book in her lap.

"You looked pretty comfortable sitting there with your eyes closed. Was that a smile on your face?" Sandra sounded so happy he was afraid to speak so he just gave her a nod. "Well I am about to find out about your secret life," and she opened the book.

Robert thought he best tell her of the emails and did so. He then added "We need to get a telephone so we may have to make a trip to civilization to set up service."

"I don't want to leave here. Not even for a few hours. For the first time in my life I feel safe. I want to sell the boat so we will have to go over there to do that and we can get a phone then. This TV series, can we handle that from here?"

He knew they would have to do some trips occasionally but he thought she is in the right place here, at least for this moment in time, and they were together. He couldn't ask for more.

"I am not sure. We will try to meet with the producer on the same trip over. Maybe I can use Donald's phone to set up the meetings. John's suggesting I bring you with me is interesting. John, and his group, don't suggest anything if it doesn't have a purpose so be prepared to be a part of anything that comes up with the TV program. Can you work with me on this if it happens. Co-writers of the manuscripts, for instance?"

Sandra looked over with a steady gaze. She was thinking hard about this. "I can work with you on anything you want to do. I will do what ever I can but it can't harm what we have right now. I mean that. I don't want to risk this," waving her hand about the area in front of them, "in any way. Is that clear?"

"That is exactly what I needed to know and exactly what I want for us," he replied.

Just as Sandra got the book opened to the first page of text Diane Connor walked up and called out a greeting. "My turn to meet Sandra. I'm Diane, otherwise know as Donald Connor's wife."

She came up to the porch and shook Sandra's hand and the bond was immediate. They talked a few minutes and then Diane noticed the big book. "What is that?"

Sandra looked at Robert and he nodded it was okay and she showed Diane the cover.

"Oh my, that is some book for Robert's adventures. I have read all three of them. Donald and I think he should keep writing the stories. They would make a good TV series," was Diane's quick response. She then took her leave, saying she was off to the grocery to pick up a few things, waving to them both as she left.

Sandra reached over and squeezed Robert's hand saying, "What nice people," and then went back to the first page.

Robert sat for a while then told Sandra he was going to see Donald about using his phone to call Alan, the boat broker, and the producer to introduce himself. That maybe he could set up the trip to see them all the same day. She nodded okay, so he was off to Donald's place. He answered the bell holding two paint brushes that were damp with paint and a harried look that told Robert he was interrupting the master at work.

"Hi Robert, what can I do for you?"

"Donald, could I borrow your phone for a few minutes. I have things to set up in San Francisco and we haven't got a phone yet." Robert felt he was interfering but he couldn't figure out how to excuse himself.

With his free hand Donald reached into his pocket and pulled out his iPhone and handed it to Robert. "I hardly ever get a call and they come to our land line as well so take this and bring it back when you are done. Keep it for a few days, just don't answer any incoming calls."

Robert's thank you was to Donald's back as he hurried back inside. He closed the door and smiled at having a friend like that. Back on the porch he told Sandra what had happened and her smile also was one of appreciation. He made the calls and the appointments were made. They would have a full day tomorrow but a lot was to be settled which would make their lives simpler and more secure. One of which was to open another door and chapter in their lives together.

Chapter 53

Sandra closed the book and looked at Robert. He was still sitting next to her on the porch with the print outs of the two emails now scribbled with notes and numbers. He looked in her direction and whispered, "Well, what do think?"

"What I think is that it is a beautifully written story. It is so good that one would think you were actually there, had just written down what happened and what was said. It's truly remarkable, Robert." Sandra was almost speechless and was struggling with what she had just experienced. "You are now going to have to tell me the story, and I mean the whole story."

"Do you want to read the other two before I try to tell you?"

"I don't have too. What I need now is to know what happened," Sandra replied without any hesitation.

"I will tell you everything that has happened. It started in the San Francisco apartment while I waited until the last minute to take my leave. I was sitting on the floor, setting up the used iPad that had arrived the day before. You remember the one I dropped off the balcony, don't you?" Robert was struggling to get this said correctly. "This was the one I bought on eBay to replace it. The one

I have now."

Sandra looked at him and a sad expression came over her face. "Yes, I remember it. It was Sunday afternoon and we were having drinks on the balcony. We were happy, Robert. we were so happy. Then on Monday the announcement was made and everything changed. I don't want to remember it. I will never forget what I did but I don't want to remember it." Her tears came and she came to Robert, put her arms around his neck and kissed him. "I am so ashamed of what I did to you. Can we just be thankful it has turned out the way it has?"

Robert returned her kiss and spoke softly "Sandra, the past sets up the future. You cannot change the past without changing the future. What would have happened with us if you had stayed with me then is not knowable now. What we do know is that it couldn't have been any better for us than it is right now. That is the only thing that matters. It couldn't have turned out better than it is right now."

"Robert, you have such a gift at making things right for me. The story can wait. All of a sudden I'm not ready to listen to anything that can spoil this moment. I can guess some of it but I know something happened that will frighten me. Let me get dinner on the table and we can start this over tonight, tomorrow or the next day. I have to know what happened eventually but it doesn't have to be now. I can wait."

"It is a long story and complicated. Nothing happened that need worry you but much of it resulted in our coming back together. That is what you need to understand. All that has happened becomes a good thing for us, and it is still happening. Don't be afraid for our future, look forward to it. We will be together and that is what I want for us and for myself."

Sandra looked at Robert, trying to smile, gave up and buried her head in his chest as he held her tight. Finally she got out in a whisper, "I am safe here with you and I love you. Please don't let anything happen that can change that."

Robert led her inside, turned on the lights and their little house was warm and dry and had a glow that made the world go away and it was just the two them together. Sandra then smiled and said. "I think that steak is ready to be fixed for dinner."

"I think you are right" and he kissed her one more time and then went out on the porch and retrieved the big Book, his iPad, Donald's phone and the two printed pages. Returning he told the beautiful cook in the kitchen, "After dinner we will plan our trip to the City."

Dinner went well and after dinner went even better. Planning for their trip to the city was left that they would have to leave early enough to be at the Chase Bank office where they were to meet Captain Alan Parsons at ten. Having that settled they fell asleep in each others arms.

It was a nice morning for a drive to San Francisco so they took the scenic route. It was always a thrill to come around a corner and see the Golden Gate Bridge, the Bay and the City on the Bay. Fighting the traffic once you descended from that view made you thank your lucky stars you didn't have to do it everyday. The meeting was good with Alan. A money transfer for the remainder of his fee was done and after a brief conversation on what a pleasurable delivery it had been, how great the boat was, and how good it was to deal with nice people Alan was off in one direction and Robert and Sandra went to meet with the boat broker.

Paul Christoff was a tall, slender gentleman who looked like he had just completed an around the world solo sail. His graying hair was just a bit shaggy and his blue eyes bright. They both liked him immediately. That was a good start. There was a little reminiscing about Conrad and that the two of them had known each other for about ten years. Paul had introduced Conrad to sailing and they had even done some racing on the Bay with a small group of friends on J-105 boats. Exciting stuff.

Paul already had a buyer for *Du-eT*. He had wanted her before Conrad bought her and he had made an offer just $20,000 less than what Conrad had paid. Paul would take only half his normal commission, which was already less than most brokers charged, since he didn't have to do anything but prep the boat, pay a months slip fee, fill the fuel tank and handle the closing documents. He looked at Sandra and said "This is a good offer. A cash deal with no contingencies from a good buyer that wants the boat and will take care of it."

Sandra didn't hesitate. "That sounds good to me. Let's do it now." Then asked, "Do you have the paperwork you need on my ownership?"

Paul smiled. "Conrad was a very thoughtful and organized man. Before you two had even left here he gave me the paper work on the co-ownership. All signed and notarized. You were a half owner, with a full ownership survivor clause, before you sailed under the Golden Gate." Some tears were shed, some of Sandra's and a few from Paul. Robert thought they must have been more than just friends, Paul and Conrad, and he said nothing. The papers were signed and a very thorough hug by Sandra and hand-shake with Robert as they left the office.

Sandra took Robert's hand as they headed back to the van. "Sometimes things work so good you don't think you deserve it. I don't think I do, but maybe we do."

It was back to the bank and Sandra opened an ac-count with a $1,000 transfer from Robert's credit card. He was given a receipt on the debit and his balance showed another $10,000 deposit had been made. Robert thought, "Sometimes things work out just perfectly."

Chapter 54

"Let's get something for lunch at Fisherman's Wharf and see if the big meeting with the producer at two o'clock goes as well." Robert tried to be positive about it. The office the meeting was to take place in was within walking distance from the Wharf so they parked in the commercial lot just off Jones Street. They shared a Fish & Chips from a take out vendor while strolling the Wharf taking in the sights and then headed for their next appointment.

The office was quite plain with only the address and door number to identify it. Sandra looked at Robert with a questioning look which he returned and shrugged his shoulders. There were two chairs so they sat down and waited. Finally Sandra asked, "What's going on, Robert?"

"I don't know. I am sure it was set for two this afternoon and it is now two fifteen. This is not exactly what I expected for a TV producer's office."

Just then the door opposite the entrance opened and a very attractive young woman entered, walked up to Robert and introduced herself. "It is a pleasure to meet you Robert Johnson. My name is Irene Carlton and I am heading the production team on Visiting History." She turned to Sandra, repeated the welcome to her and then asked them both to come with her. The door Irene had come in from led to a long hallway which was a considerable improvement over the reception area and entering Irene's office was enough to make you think twice about first impressions. Grand came to Robert's mind.

"Please be seated," was offered and Sandra and Robert sank into luxurious leather. "We are going to discuss a little on how we are approaching this project, what we hope to do, and what we need from you. As you might expect, John has been somewhat involved and is actually financially part of our organization. You may also anticipate he won't be further involved beyond this point. I have only met him once and that meeting was short and efficient. I know nothing about him, or his businesses, just that he approached us on the idea of a TV series that could be successful and profitable. Our staff read your manuscripts, bound by the way in a beautiful leather portfolio cover, and we concurred. His agent, whom we haven't met in person, set some terms on your contribution to make this project viable and we again concurred."

Irene Carlton paused, giving both Robert and Sandra a knowing smile, and then continued.

"All that is required from you, and I assume from both of you, is six more manuscripts in a matching format and quality, one every two weeks, for the next twelve weeks. This will ensure a season of one hour length shows which we can promote to a network. You will receive ten thousand dollars per manuscript and have a two and a half percent royalty on every airing of a show based on our profit. The royalty can vary from nothing to a considerable amount of money depending on the popularity of the shows. You have no liability of any kind. That is important," Irene paused to let this sink in. Then she sealed the deal with, "John wants me to tell you that his agent has already signed the papers and he suggest you do the same. That is all he said. It is a strange way to do business but this is show business."

Robert was stunned and Sandra looked scared to death. Irene said she would step out of the office and they could discuss the offer.

"Well that was efficient. It looks pretty good. I was prepared for doing the six manuscripts and have done preparations already. I don't see that as a problem. John wrote that he would have an agent work on my behalf and I can accept the two and a half percent royalty as a good number. He also said I could have you work with me but that would be up to us to splitting up the remuneration. There is an income tax angle there of course." Robert had covered the bases but wasn't sure he touched them all. Sandra sat stunned.

"I will go with you anywhere you want go, Robert. If you are comfortable with it sign on the dotted line and let's go home. That is where I want to be right now." Sandra finished with moving to his chair and sitting on the arm rest placing her hand on his shoulder and giving him a light massage.

Robert told her "I trust John so I am going to sign up. I like doing the writing and you can help with the research and editing. You may like the work and we can make it an enjoyable team effort. Is that okay with you?"

"Yes."

Irene Carlton came back in and positioned the papers on her desk facing them and indicated where Robert should sign them. He did and she quickly made three copies, collated them and stapled each together. She paper clipped a check to Robert's and placed it in a folder and and handed it to him. Then stuck out her hand and shook Robert's offered one. "That was quick and totally unusual for putting together a project like this. John must have some kind of magic. Robert, you have just made the deal of a lifetime. If this works out you will be nicely rewarded for years to come. This has been a pleasure."

Five minutes later they were in the van. Robert handed Sandra the folder. She opened the folder and smiled. "Let's get to work, partner. Does thirty thousand dollars sound about right?"

"Yes"

Robert slid his credit card in the parking lot's kiosk and it took out thirty-two dollars from his account and gave him his card back. They would go the faster route back with a stop at the shopping mall in San Rafael getting their new phones at a Verizon store and buying a Dell laptop for Sandra at Best Buy. They were home by six and glad to be there. It had been an excellent trip to the City.

Chapter 55

After dinner Robert and Sandra took the short walk they were making a routine and talked about the day and how smoothly everything had gone. Robert then made a comment that Sandra picked up on immediately. "It went too smoothly. Everything was just too easy, like it was all planned out for us. But how could that be. Alan, Paul, Irene are all totally unrelated in business. Alan and Paul may know each other but are not friends and Irene doesn't know either of them."

They continued walking and finally Sandra got to the point. "I need to know what happened on your visits. How they came about and who is John? He is involved in all of this, isn't he? Did he buy *Du-eT*, Jerry and Julie's house and their station? Is he funding you so far? Did he have some connection with Conrad? Questions, questions, questions and why this is happening is the big one? Let's start with you telling me what happened at the apartment and every day until we saw each other in Campbell River."

After they got back to the house they sat opposite each other on the small dining table chairs. Robert laid out the three visit manuscripts on the table with his iPad adjusted as it was when he took the visit trips. He set it so

Sandra could see the screen and started his story. "That afternoon in the apartment, the day I had to vacate, I had a few hours left and decided to set up my new iPad. Once I had downloaded what I wanted this strange looking Icon showed up in the lower right corner." He pointed out to where it had been, said that he had touched it, and then continued describing the message. "You have the chance to visit history as it is happening. Do you have the courage to go there?" Adding that it was in blood red script.

Sandra gasped and stuttered out, "Oh my God! What did you do?"

"I touched the enter button and an agreement page came up. I skipped over it and was about touch the agree button when a message came up using my full birth name Herbert Robert Johnson." Nobody, and I mean nobody, knows me by Herbert. Nobody. I read the agreement and decided I would think about it later. I told you what happened next and how I ended up in this house in Point Reyes Station. But I left out one detail."

Sandra was beginning to think she may not want to hear it. "Wait a minute, do I want to know this?"

Robert took her hands in his and told her "You will have to know but just understand it was here but isn't now and never will be again. It was just some common material that had been installed and was removed when I was headed up to help you. Our bedroom had been converted into a sound proof room, the walls, windows, ceiling and door. All sound proofed." Robert felt her tense up and her grip on his hands tightened.

She then started to really looked scared. "That has something wrong with the timing. How did they know you would stay here. Even stop in Point Reyes Station?"

"They didn't know but they were able to predict it might happen. You can guess what I was thinking when I saw that room because in the agreement pages was a description of the kind of space I would need on a visit. This room was exactly what was required."

"Robert I don't want hear any more. Not right now. It is frightening to think that could be done."

"You need to know a little more before we stop for tonight. I was having internet contact once I agreed to participate. It was what to expect, the low level of risk of traveling back in time, the rules when there and even a question of who I would like to visit. I choose Lincoln as you have just read about. But first was a delivery of some high tech ear devices, a transmitter/receiver module and a battery charger. All miniaturized."

Sandra was now intent on his every word so he continued. "I confided with Donald and he knows about every detail. When I decided to do the first trip, which was decided by them and would be a ten minute demonstration, Donald would wait on the porch to make sure I returned intact."

Sandra interrupted with "How could you take such a risk? Not coming back, how could you do such a thing?"

Robert wasn't sure he should tell her but he did. "At the time I didn't think I had any thing to lose."

"Oh no Robert, don't say that. Please not because of me." Her tears came but Robert knew this was the moment he needed.

"Sandra the first trip was one of the greatest experiences I have ever had. It was ten minutes with my mother and father as we toured the MIT campus on my first day in the Fall of 1994. It was so real. They were happy, young, my mother so pretty and my father handsome. We talked and toured exactly as we had done that day twenty-one years ago. The colors were vivid and we talked and laughed just like we had then. Then suddenly it was over, I was staring at the iPad and started crying like a baby. There was no way I would not try another visit into history."

Sandra had dried her tears and then started to look at Robert directly. She could see he meant what he had said and the thought of being able to do something like this would have an appeal. "But it has to be dangerous. This has to do with your mind, your brain, not your body. Was it dangerous?"

"Yes, in a way. I was able to do the three trips that are written up. The ones you get to read. On return from the Lincoln visit I had a little dizziness, coming back from the da Vinci it was a little more severe and the return from Rachmaninoff it was bad. We decided that was all the trips that would be safe for me to take."

Sandra said, "That's enough! I think I understand but I don't see how it can be done. If anyone other than you would tell me such a story I would laugh at them. I want you to take me to bed now and hold me until I fall asleep. We can talk some more tomorrow. You do understand?"

"Yes I do. Sandra, it was a life changing event. And what is happening now is giving me a new life to live and you are with me to live it. That is all I can ask."

Chapter 56

Tomorrow came as did the next few weeks. Sandra read the other two manuscripts and came away with the same sense that they were extraordinary documents that should be shared. She had no questions. She knew what had happened and didn't, as did Robert, care how it had been possible. They discussed the TV Project and started to formulate how they could work together. It started with that familiar search at the Thrift Shop for a work table and they found a used Danish style six foot drop leaf supported by four plain dowel shaped legs. Another office chair was also available and both were purchased. The small bedroom was to be the office and against one wall was the table and and two chairs side by side. The single bed was pushed against the other wall and with bolsters would act as a sofa. With the table leaves up it provided a large flat surface and soon had both laptops and the printer in place and a box of printer paper on the floor underneath. Robert hooked up an over head light fixture and the office, Visiting History, was in place.

From the list of possibles Robert had put together he choose John Locke, the English philosopher and physician, who's work in the late 1600's guided the founders of the Declaration of Independence, the United States Constitution, and influenced Adam Smith who in essence developed what became the economic system of Capitalism. Robert liked this choice. In his father's library were several books about Locke and a Smith's *Wealth of Nations.* When they had the room to their liking, Robert and Sandra sat in the chairs, looked at the blank screens of their laptops, then at each other and started to smile and then laugh. Sandra said "Well boss, what do we do now?"

"First it is partner, not boss. Here is my plan to start. I will make a transcript like was provided me from John's group of the conversations of my visits only this time I will of course make them up. You, my partner, will research John Locke and find out as much as you can on appearance, habits, idiosyncrasies, personal life, home and office, or rooms, where he worked. We need a date and time of day for the visit and most important a location. Then we will try to merge our two efforts into something like my previous visits were documented. It is that merging that a lot of give and take between us will have to take place. Let's agree right now that we agree to disagree without personal affront. What do you think?"

Sandra gave Robert what he now called "the smile" and turned on her laptop.

The fourth of July came and Point Reyes had a small firework's display which was set up by the volunteer fire department. Most of the town participated and a number of tourist and visitors showed up. It was well attended in a small town way and it was just right as far as Robert and Sandra were concerned. The Connors and Gallagers joined them on a blanket in the field over looking the marsh area where the fireworks were ignited. Donald and Diane had become their close friends and they had almost adopted Sandra as a daughter. On a later day Donald set up a trap shoot and the four of them shot a hundred clays each. Sandra was a natural and would carry the load for Robert. For the next season a pheasant hunt was being planned. Dinners at each others homes were being exchanged and life was becoming comfortable.

The small box from the mortuary in Campbell River had arrived and the attractive urn was placed on the top of the bookcase. Sandra had tried to put the inevitable out of her mind but it was now unavoidable. Robert also was moved by the finality of one's life and that it could end in such a small container. Both his mother and father had chosen cremation and he now had that same feeling of sadness he had with their final disposition. He described to Sandra the small clearing he had found on his hike in the Point Reyes National Seashore. What a peaceful and beautiful place it was and that it would be what Conrad would have wanted.

With moist eyes she asked, "Is that allowed there, the scattering of ashes?"

"Probably not but who was to know. It is a big area and the view of the Pacific and of the beaches below is magnificent. There are acres and acres of hillside grasses and small shrubs and trees. We will find the perfect spot."

"Let's do it tomorrow. I will never forget Conrad, but he belongs somewhere like that and I need to believe he will be there in spirit," Sandra spoke with some relief at the thought.

The next afternoon was as good as an afternoon could be. The sky was clear and so blue it almost hurt the eyes. A gentle breeze made the three mile hike comfortable and when Robert found his small clearing Sandra thought it perfect. They wandered around the area and on a small knoll with the perfect view Conrad's ashes were scattered. Sandra came over to Robert, stood close and whispered "Thank you." They took a last look and said their goodbyes to a special person who had touched their lives in such important ways.

Chapter 57

The first manuscript was delivered and enthusiastically received on July fifteenth. Sandra was a great researcher and had adapted to providing just what was needed in fleshing out the character of John Locke such that Robert could write up the visit effortlessly. It was a much bigger task than the previous three as there was very little personal information available. Most was centered around his academic papers, where they were written and why he was there. He never married. His last nine years were spent at Lord and Lady Masham's country home Oates, near Essex. It was there he died in 1704. Lady Masham, Abigail, thirty-eight years his junior was interestingly very involved in his life for some years.

Robert chose his visit to be at Oates in Fall of 1702. The visit was of course entirely fictionalized but still resulted in a fun read and a good examination of a major force of the enlightenment. Their partnership was going to work. It was not only enjoyable, the work shared brought them even closer together.

In the afternoon two days later, on Friday, the seventeenth of July, a car looking just like every other car on the road pulled up in front of the little house that the Gallagers had once owned, just two blocks from the gas station they had also once owned, and on the front porch which was where Robert and Sandra were then sitting.

A rather short man got out, stretched, and came around the car and walked up to the porch. He was maybe five foot-ten and about one hundred sixty-five pounds. He had hair that could be described as gray and whose clothes were beige in color. His eyes were blue, or maybe blue green with just a hint of brown. The eyes you would remember, however, not by their color but as they sparkled with intelligence and humor. But later, the rest you would not be able to describe. He looked at them on the porch and said, "It is good to meet you both. Robert and Sandra, my name is John."

John pulled up the offered chair, the three of them forming a triangle, knees almost touching. His leather shoes had just a slight covering of dust and were of a modern style walking type. His pants and shirt cotton of a good weave and texture. He wore a leather belt with an open weave and silver buckle of a simple but unique design. His watch could have been a Seiko or a Rolex. He had good teeth, but not Hollywood white, and he wore no cologne or after shave lotion. You could not even tell whether he was just nicely dressed or in the most expensive clothes obtainable. At the time neither Robert or Sandra paid the least attention.

The next half hour was one of the most interesting that either Robert or Sandra would ever spend. John told them the story starting the day Robert accepted the job at Engstrum Technologies and continued on with the day Sandra met Robert at the San Francisco apartment rental showing. He was relaxed, totally at ease and he started with the first of many revelations.

"You should first know that myself and five friends are a venture capital group who have done extremely well ever since Silicon Valley became Silicon Valley. We made our first big killing in 1972. From then on it has been one big winner after another with very few missteps. Next, we funded Engstrum Technology. You may think that was a misstep, Robert, but I will get to that in a minute. Your hire at Engstrum's was noted and Conrad gave us a heads up on you. Don't be surprised but you do have some attributes that we look for. Understand, Conrad had no idea that we put you on a keeper list. Engstrum Technologies was so close to making the breakthrough you were looking for that we felt guilty letting your funding run out when it didn't work out. We had detected another direction you could have gone but we knew we could easily get there with another group and not share in the profits."

Robert didn't know what to say to that so he didn't say anything. John looked at Robert and said, "That is what attracted us to you, Robert. You are one of the few who knows when to wait for the answer and not ruin the chance of getting it by speaking too soon. The answer is that your group had the answer but it was not what you were looking for and therefore you couldn't see it. In your visits, and in our instructions, is the fact that you could speak in English and your subject would understand and respond in English, like Leonard da Vinci did, without knowing any English. Did that not impress you?"

Robert almost fell off his chair. "I worked on that and we had a technician working on several possibilities but we never found the right combination to make it viable. It was a side effort to make the use of our program international without always having interpreters around. You did it! You must have because on the visit with da Vinci it worked flawlessly. Devices like that would make you millions."

John chuckled. "They have already. About the size of an iPhone with ear devices the same as those you used. Da Vinci was speaking in an Italian dialect and your English was being converted to his language and his to English in real time from our laboratory. How that is done you will probably never really understand but it does work and the use of human interpreters is just about over."

"How we do the visits I will not discuss. We will still be working on this but not with humans again for a while. I did tell you after Rachmaninoff that you were actually our only traveler other than very short visits our members took. Maybe some time in the future we will see if we can monetize the technology but we have enough data now to proceed with experiments of a different kind."

"Now back to March 31, this year. The iPad was a simple task. We picked up your eBay purchase and provided you with our own. You still have the same one but all that we had loaded into it has been removed. It was integral in setting up the visits and help guide you to Point Reyes Station. We knew about Jerry Gallager's problem with getting help. Turning on your gas warning light was not a problem and knowing your disposition and emotional state we knew that if you met Jerry at the right moment it would work out with the house. Preparing the sound proof room was a risk but not an expensive one. It was unfair to use some subliminal persuasion but we are good at that and most times, just like in this case, it works. Now we also must admit your iPad, and the previous one, had been bugged as was your Porsche and the apartment. Your meeting Sandra and her entry into the picture was entirely random. We only monitored your relationship in the living room and the car. No where else."

There was a pause and neither Robert or Sandra wanted to interfere.

John continued. "Let's get you to the present. First understand, Robert, we were interested in you on a number of levels. We are still interested but until the TV Series is developed and runs it's course it is such a good fit for you and Sandra we will not interfere in any way. We have retracted all monitoring in your personal life. I should also note that we had worked with Conrad for a number of years. You already discovered that he had little public history before his company was started and that is because he had worked for us on several secret projects. He was such a good man that losing him that way was a very sad thing. We had nothing to do with Sandra's choices but she definitely made his last months on earth much better than they would have been otherwise. We know how important it was to him."

John knew he had said something that was problematic for Sandra so he quickly jumped to the house. "About the little house right here. Yes, we bought it and the station. We paid top dollar for both, and it was probably too much, but we needed you to stay in place for our visiting history project. Sandra being gone was in no way planned for and was definitely not coordinated with Conrad. We had nothing to do with *Du-eT* in either it's purchase, sale, or use. We did make the two deposits to your credit card, Robert, and consider that a salary benefit for services rendered. The TV production company is under our umbrella of holdings but is operated independently and your success or failure is in their hands and yours. Our lawyers looked over the contract, think it is a good one for you and is in no way out of line for a project like this. And by the way, John Locke is approved and a spin off for school class broadcasts are already in the planning stage."

John sat back. "Well what do think? Has it worked out all right for you two so far? Oh yes, the little house right here in Point Reyes Station. It is yours to use rent free until January 31, 2016. At that time we can set up a rental or sales agreement. They will both be below market value if you choose either. As you are aware, this is a very expensive area real estate wise. You will have to decide on whatever is best for you at that time. I wouldn't count out, however, very successful writing careers for you both."

John stood up not waiting for answers to his questions. He knew what they would be so waiting was unnecessary. They shook hands warmly, saying goodbyes, and the rather small man with exceedingly sharp eyes that may have been blue, or blue green with a touch of brown, got into his ordinary car and drove away.

Robert and Sandra stood silently on the porch, arms around each others waist, watching the small black, or was it gray, car turn at the corner and disappear from view.

Sandra turned towards Robert, looked directly into his eyes, and told him, "He will be back into our lives someday. John will definitely be back. No matter what his reason, plans or purpose, I will be with you then and I will join you in whatever you decide to do. No matter what!"

About The Author

Art Myers was born in 1935 and grew up in the small southern California town of La Mesa. He graduated from San Diego State College in 1958 with a BS Degree in Engineering. Several employments in the Military Industrial Complex lasted until end of 1969. His first layoff was in 1961 and he spent the fall months working as construction labor in Mammoth Lakes, CA and the winter of 1962 skiing in Aspen, CO. Another stint in engineering and a second layoff occurred which found him with a wife, daughter, house payments and just beginning what became a 30 year career as a professional sculptor. Interspersed in that 30 years were a variety of residences and occupations for both he and his wife. Retiring in 2002 they bought a sail boat and spent 10 years living aboard and cruising both US coasts. They have lived in a variety of places including Saratoga, CA, Aspen and Loveland, CO, Lake Forest, IL and currently in Vero Beach, FL. His first book was an autobiography written for family and friends in 2015. "A New Life for Robert Johnson" is his second work of fiction, 2019.

www.ingramcontent.com/pod-product-compliance
Lightning Source LLC
Chambersburg PA
CBHW070524100726
47907CB00004B/967